Rose Petals

Liz Crowe

The songs mentioned in the story named *Pretty In Blue* and *Ladybird* are fictional songs and not based on any real songs written or recorded at the time of publication.

This is a work of fiction. Names, characters, organisations, places, events, and incidents are either products of the author's imagination or are used fictitiously. Any resemblance to actual persons, living or dead, or actual events is purely coincidental.

Interior design and layout by Crowerotica Fantasies.

Chapter One

"Turn that fucking mike on, will ya…"

I glance up over the backs of the chairs—surprised—when someone unfamiliar calls out at the top of her lungs. Laughter follows the demand from another direction. A husky laughter of a man who definitely smokes more than is good for him. I chuckle under my breath when the woman yells out once more, "You fucking moron, stop bitching about and do what I said…"

I squint my eyes and stare into the darkness of where the laughter had come from, then a nudge distracts me.

"Tash, I asked you which song you would sing tomorrow?"

I glance at Mick, my boyfriend of four years. His sneering grin shows he'd heard the other woman yelling too. And also that he'd heard the other guy laughing as a reaction. He snickers under his breath commenting, "I don't think she needs that fucking mike by the sounds of it. Maybe call out and tell them to shut up…"

"Why should I?"

I glare at Mick, feeling annoyed at his comment.

"She's competition. Don't you realise that? And that person she yelled at seems more of a stalker…"

"I ain't here to win. I just want to prove to myself that I can sing in front of a large audience."

"Maybe wear your swimsuit and your cowboy hat alone," Mick says. "It will distract—"

He cringes from my slap. Not a hard slap, but it's one of those slaps to shut a person up.

"I want to win because people appreciate my skill of singing," I hiss angrily.

"Then why do you keep looking at her?" Mick asks, nodding sidelong towards the other woman below them who seems to be in a tirade of arguing with the man who keeps laughing at it from time to time.

"I'm just curious why she's letting him talk at her in this way…" I grunt.

"Hmm, is that right?" Mick asks, now also staring at the woman, though I notice him lusting at her.

"Eyes front, mister," I grunt, pulling his face towards me.

"Yes, ma'am," he says bluntly, smirking ever so slightly. His eyes flick sideways like he's still trying to look at the other woman on the podium.

"Let's just ignore them," I say, and then after I pick up the sheet of paper listing song suggestions on it I add softly, "I just want to survive this weekend. You know how my parents view my career choice of singing…"

"That's one thing I'm disgusted about in the way they speak to you," Mick comments. "That's *why* I want you to succeed here…"

"If I don't succeed over here, I can go to the other one for another chance…"

"It feels you're moving to goal posts when you say that," Mick mumbles. "Don't let them…"

I look up at him and silently nod.

Mick takes hold of my face and he stares into my eyes before he whispers, "Tash, you know I love you, right?"

I nod curtly before turning my attention back to the paperwork on the floor in front of me.

"I love you—too," I whisper. Suddenly whether I really love Mick was bothering my mind again. Especially since he'd introduced me to his 'kink' and I was certain that he's eyeing up the woman yelling at her manager, or boyfriend, or whatever down below us for the 'kink.'

"Can you *stop* looking at her already…?" I ask. "She might be married to that guy for all we know."

Mick grunts, and with a renewed smirk he voices what's on his mind now, "Maybe he has a similar interest—"

"I ain't going to fuck some stranger to satisfy your—"

"Only if they're like us…"

"You mean like you," I say, laughing now.

"Are you saying you're not into it suddenly?"

"I'm more interested in winning this competition… or at a minimum to be in the shortlist," I say.

"Hmm, okay. But don't you want some fun while we wait?"

"Not in that way…" I snap.

"Fine, fine…" he says. "Maybe I should just go to the bar and see what they're serving up later for lunch."

"Oh fine, go then," I say. "I'd have some peace then. I bet you'll be drunk before dinner."

Mick chuckles somewhat, then he says solemnly, "Which gets me more horny. It will give you a night of good sex in bed later, don't you remember that, huh…?"

"You're saying that to distract me…"

"Am I succeeding?"

I glance up and stare at his pleased smirk. He found me out with my simple response. I feel my cheeks heat and a warm feeling rising through my body. I feel awkward suddenly as I had showed off my athletic skills to sit down with each leg in either direction. It exposes me to Mick's next motion. He leans forward like he will kiss me. Instead, his hand reaches for my crotch. I moan suddenly from his expert rubbing motion that turns me on through the layer of jeans and panties. Then he kisses and, for several minutes, I forget all about the upcoming rehearsals…

After twenty minutes of Mick kissing me and playing with his hand inside my panties, I push him away from me and slide down so I'm lying down, and with a muffled moan I arch up towards him. He has my jeans unbuttoned in a swift motion and both my jeans and panties are halfway down my legs in the next motion. I lift one leg and I lie there naked from waist down; well, except for my panties and jeans that are crumpled around my right leg.

Mick leans down and kisses my belly gently, then in a play of further kisses he arrives at my pussy, and flicks his tongue over my clit. I cover my mouth with both hands to muffle my groan. He makes it hard to keep my moans quiet by licking my clit and then looks up at me grinning broadly. He leans over me, kissing my lips, and he's unzipping his own jeans. A moment later he inserts his hard dick inside my pussy. I moan loudly.

"Shush," he whispers. "They'll hear you otherwise…"

I chuckle, and glance sideways, and check under the seats towards the podium. It's empty…

"They're gone," I hiss.

"Dammit…" Mick groans. "I wanted to annoy them by hearing us fucking…"

I giggle then I suggest, "I wanted it too now…"

Mick grins at me and asks, "So you like my kinks?"

I nod.

The admission to 'like' Mick's kinks suddenly makes him more horny—obviously. He pulls his dick back and slams it into my pussy harder. Rough sex has always been my kink, even if I've never told this to Mick. I'm certain that he suspects this to be the case. But nothing compares to his supposed kink, which he almost had admitted to a few minutes earlier. His kink is a boyfriend swap, meaning that he'd fuck some other girl, and that girl's boyfriend would fuck me at the same time. Even more so if it allowed the two boyfriends to see the other girl and me make out at the same time. Meaning she and I would indulge is some lesbian kissing or even possibly playing with each other's pussy while they fucked us. It was exciting me now, and suddenly I knew the perfect girl to persuade into such actions.

I close my eyes and imagine the dark-haired woman who'd screamed at the top of her lungs for such a boyfriend swap.

If she has that ability of yelling, how does she sound while someone is fucking her? I think. *The 'someone fucking' would be Mick. I could watch him fuck her…*

I moan loudly and don't even attempt to hide it I'm enjoying the lovemaking. Suddenly, with a new plan in my mind, it doesn't matter if I'm heard. *I want her to hear this. If that's her manager, she probably will feel jealous that she can't have fun in this way…*

A warm stream deep inside me tells me that my moaning has caused Mick's orgasm. Another couple of pushes and it's over…

Mick stares at me for a minute, then unexpectedly he moves lower, and he's licking my pussy once more…

+++

An hour later and we're lying side by side on the hard floor and each time we look at one another we burst out in a fit of laughter that we quickly try to subdue as the voice of the other woman calls out yet another complaint aimed at the guy who now seems to have had enough of her behaviour and shouts out some choice swear words at her.

Both of us cover our mouths tightly with our hands. Listening to two people quarrelling is maybe not the best way to pass time, but it stirs a new idea in my mind and I have to admit it's probably my kink.

Mick turns his head to peer between the legs of the chairs at the woman on the podium; it's obvious he's filling his mind with many ideas on how to get the other woman and me in the same bed for his other form of kinds. I lift my head and stare past him and try to guess her age. If Mick has an idea forming in his head, I didn't want to end up a bed with a girl. A woman of my age—someone like me who is in her early twenties—would be worth my while. But as I stare, an idea forms in my mind. An idea where I could get my sweet revenge for all the times I had to take part so brutally in all of Mick's kinks over the last three years; at least that's how long I've known about Mick's kinks…

Perhaps I can get her to help me with this plan. Maybe I can get her to use some of her skill of performing to create a situation that benefits her and me rather than Mick or that loser of a guy she keeps yelling at. I stare at Mick's head and smile maliciously for a moment. *Maybe she can help me teach Mick a lesson or two. Not that the sex just now was bad. I just want it on my terms from time to time.*

"I need to use the bathroom," I say abruptly.

Mick's jerks his gaze towards me, nods once, then his gaze is immediately back towards her. *What's so appealing him about her? I don't think he'd go after her if he was single…*

I get up and pull up my panties. After tucking my clothing back into some order fashion, I lean down for my bag. As I do this, I feel Mick's hand slide up over my left leg until it comes to a rest just beside my panties. A finger slides inside my panties, and I groan involuntarily as his finger slides back and forth over my clit.

"Stop it," I hiss. "I need to use the bathroom…"

"Come back fast or I'll chat her up," Mick grunts.

Looking down at him, I see a playful smile curl his lips. It broadens as he slides his finger deep inside my pussy. I close my eyes a moment and let my mind savour the feeling of his finger inside. A fuzzy feeling overwhelms me and for a few moments I feel tempted to just lower myself to the floor and let him have his way with me.

"I need to—I have to go," I stammer. "They will be—stop it, please…"

"I can wait…" Mick grunts curtly and makes it harder for me to leave by inserting a second finger alongside the first, and by making me horny to the bone. Then his fingers are gone and I feel almost disappointed by his actions.

I walk off without saying a word and not even looking back, but I feel that he's staring after me now and is undressing me as I speed up my departure. At the exit door I glance towards him to see him once more staring towards the other woman, and I can guess he's now undressing her with the same intensity he did just now with me.

A moment later the other woman disappears from sight, and I exit into the unlit corridor before Mick can shift his attention back to me again.

Once in the corridor I look in both directions, and now the urge for using the toilet replaces the still lingering sensations of Mick's actions only moments ago.

Just as I spot the sign for the restroom a hundred yards away, a sound startles me and I quickly rush towards the restroom. I was not in the mood for sex with Mick in this corridor where anyone could just walk in on us…

Chapter Two

Dammit, Mick, you and your kinks. I'm getting fed up of them really. Maybe it's time for some kinks of my own choosing. Maybe I should just lock myself away in the restrooms until it's past lunch time and the rehearsals start…

Once I'm in the cubicle in the restroom, I lean back against the wall behind me. I'm startled for a moment by the sensation of flowing water spraying in the toilet when I accidentally hit the automated flushing button. This adds a new sensation to every other feeling going through my body.

I close my eyes and my hand slides towards my wet pussy—it's wet from the water that had just sprayed up below me as I flushed. My fingers slide over my clit, and I savour a few moments of renewed hot waves going through all of my body. My finger slides into my pussy, and it causes my body to arch. My other hand grasps my boob, and a moment later pulls at my nipple.

My mouth opens involuntarily, and a moment later I'm groaning softly. This is my sort of kink. I love playing with my pussy whenever I'm alone…

The repeated flushing of water as my head brushes over the automatic button causes my pussy and ass to be wet through after just three flushes.

"Hey, cut it out with the damned flushing, will ya… I'm trying to work on my lyrics here…"

I jerk upright and stare to my left.

The voice that just spoke belongs to the woman I'd been watching downstairs in the concert hall.

"Sorry, I'm trying to wash myself…" I say bluntly.

Laughter from a few yards away. Then she points out the obvious, "There are shower cubicles in the room next door. If you want to wash go there, you idiot."

"It's my first time here. I didn't know about them…" I say.

"I guess you can't read the signage above the door beside the door to this restroom…" she says before laughing loudly. "But to be honest, by the sound of how the flushing was going it sounded more like you were pleasuring yourself… am I right?"

"So what if I do that?"

More laughter from her.

"When you're not doing whatever it is you're doing in there, why are you here?" she asks.

"I'm here for the rehearsals."

"Singing or watching it?" she asks.

"Singing."

"I guess we can compare who sings better later on…"

She now giggles incessantly. I wait until it subsides before I comment.

"If my boyfriend has any say in it, I will never sing," I grunt. "He thinks being here is a waste of time. A waste of his time to be precise…"

"It sounds your boyfriend is as much a pain in the butt as my one is…"

Now it's my turn to laugh before I comment, "Was the guy I heard you yell at your boyfriend?"

"You guessed right," she says. "I guess you were somewhere in the rafters watching me…"

"About halfway up the auditorium. I was busy with my boyfriend there…" I answer.

"Busy, huh? I can guess by the sound of your activities here that he didn't give you enough attention…" she comments then without pausing she adds, "What's your name, anyway?"

"Tash," I answer.

"Just Tash? Or is that short for something else?" she asks.

"Blame my overzealous hippy mother to give me THAT name," I grunt. "It's just Tash…"

"In case you're remotely interested, my name is Suzie," she says. "Giving to me by my boring, not-so-hippy mother…"

Both of us burst out laughing loudly.

After a few minutes pausing the conversation, she suggests the best possible idea I'd heard all day, "Let's grab lunch…"

+++

A few minutes later, we stand staring at one another from either end of the restroom. I'm certain she's scrutinising me thoroughly. It's not likely many women wearing a cowboy hat, unkempt hair, no makeup came to town. Compared to me she was a spotless beauty—dark pink glossy lipstick, eyes caked with eyeshadow and eyeliner, powdered face, her hair brushed to perfection. The contrast was plainly obvious. I could see why Mick had been watching her before…

"Do I meet your approval?" Suzie asks coldly.

"I wish they can brush my hair to perfection like yours can be," I answer, unfazed by the coldness in her voice. "But if an opinion matters, you look great…"

A faint smile appears on Suzie's face.

"I'm being honest. I wish I had your hair, and I wish I was half as good with makeup," I say bluntly.

"Why no makeup?" Suzie asks.

"Mick doesn't let me use it…" I reply.

"Mick?"

"My boyfriend," I answer.

"Ah right, so he's as much of a control freak as my one is…" Suzie says.

"I guess so."

"And the reason you decided to…?" Suzie asks, smiling maliciously and nodding towards the cubicles. "Is he a prude, and that's why you had to…?"

"If you really need to know we had sex in the auditorium while you were yelling at that guy…" I blurt out.

"That guy is my boyfriend," Suzie snaps before laughing loudly. "And he IS a prude…"

"Oh, how come?" I ask gleefully.

Suzie is right in front of me in a few steps, and before I know it she has grabbed my face and kisses me on my lips. But somehow I don't mind she's doing it. The sensation of a woman kissing me gives me an intriguing sensation. I feel myself responding to her kisses, and only a moment later I've pulled her closer towards me. Just a few seconds longer, then she pushes herself away from me.

We stare at one another for several minutes. It's obvious the behaviour left us both tongue-tied. We grin broadly at each other moments later, both amused at what had just happened.

"I was testing you…" Suzie says.

"Testing me?" I ask. "How? For what?"

"How well you respond to pretence…" Suzie says. "I ain't a lesbian if you wondered that."

"I ain't one either," I blurt out.

"But… you liked it?"

I nod. Oddly enough, I did enjoy the sensations it had given me.

"I wonder… Would you want to have your own bit of fun? To teach my prude boyfriend some stuff about sex?" Suzie asks.

"Like a ménage à trois?" I ask.

"Naah, more like YOU teach my prude boyfriend to want sex, and if you want it, I could in turn entertain your boyfriend… hmmm… let's call it repaying the 'watching me' from earlier," Suzie says. "There are some dark areas in the rafters above the podium. They'd never know that I'm with your boyfriend, and that you are with my loser boyfriend…"

I'm tongue-tied again for another reason. My pussy tells me it agrees with the 'plan' suggested by Suzie. She smirks, and it's obvious that she knows my answer will be a resounding 'yes.'

Suzie saunters closer until she's almost standing against me again. Her hand moves up and brushes through my hair, then her hand caresses over my cheek, slowly it lowers and rests over my boob for several minutes. She stares at me, sensually smiles at me before her smile broadens.

My eyes widen when I feel her other hand slide down inside my skirt and is pulling at the edge of my panties. After her hand tickles over my skin, it slides down inside my panties. Suzie's hand cups my pubic hair, brushing her fingers up and down for a few minutes. Her fingers travel down and rub over my clit. I gasp when her finger slides inside my pussy…

+++

The experience of 'almost' having a lesbian encounter with Suzie lasts just a matter of minutes. I struggle with not moaning loudly. She just stares at me with a chiselled expression on her face. I'm guessing she's testing my resolve to see if I would be able to pull off her 'plan' of fooling her boyfriend. A hint of a smirk that plays on the side of her mouth indicates that she enjoys this encounter and perhaps is looking forward to the execution of the plan. It sounds like something that might belong in some sort of movie plot if I think it through more thoroughly. IF I can think between the surges of orgasm coming from my pussy being rubbed by her finger…

Then suddenly her hand is gone. A hand covers my mouth and softly, almost sensually, she murmurs, "Shh… Someone will hear you…"

My pussy throbs from the orgasm I'd just experienced. Not even Mick has ever managed to pleasure me so intensely or so abruptly. But SHE did…

"What the hell did you do it?" I hiss at her.
"To see if you could pull off the plan I just laid out to you," Suzie says calmly. "Don't you want to have your own revenge on your boyfriend for insisting on sex with him in the auditorium?"
I nod plainly.
"I guess he often gets his own way of how sex goes, right?"
I nod again.
"With me it's the total opposite. My loser boyfriend wants no sex at all," Suzie grunts. "I'm lucky if I get some at least once every other month. His excuse… too busy being my manager to care about such trivialities…"

"Trivialities?" I ask.

"That's how he refers to it…" Suzie blurts out, frowning angrily now. "He gets his kicks from annoying me to hell and back."

"So what was that stuff about, anyway? When I heard you yell at him?" I ask.

"He likes to pretend I can't sing…" Suzie smiles wryly at me before she turns on the tap and washes her hands. "He claims I have no business being in this concert. He claims it's an event for losers…"

"Let me hear you sing…" I blurt out, and a moment later I stare in amazement when Suzie belts out my favourite song; which happens to be a song by Lady Gaga. I shake my head to dismiss my thought. I want to concentrate on her ability to sing, not the reasons for her to belt out this particular song.

"Do you write your own songs?" I ask next.

She nods curtly, but from the lip biting I can tell it's a contentious topic.

"Sing something…" I whisper hesitantly.

Suzie looks at me for a moment, then she sighs deeply then in her next breath she has captured my heart. Not in a reaction of the lesbian encounter from just moments earlier, but because her voice went from belting out to a timbre that might easily have belonged to a different person. The sound of her 'a cappella' - to coin the wording I had learnt in music school - was so perfect that the restroom manages to echo her singing back at us and it sounds more like there are four or five of her singing right now. It lasts only a minute or so then she's silent…

"That sounded so beautiful…" I whisper. "Why doesn't he want you singing that way?"

"He likes punk rock. He wants me to be singing in that way…" Suzie says coldly. "I wish I could go with this option in the concert…"

"Hmm, I guess your contractual obligations prevent you from sacking him?" I ask.

Suzie nods.

"And the boyfriend part? Where does that fit into it all?" I ask.

"He wants me to take a stage name," Suzie says. "He wants me to do this career he has all mapped out for me as… Please don't laugh… as 'Rose Petals'…"

I gape at her. More from shock than anything else.

"You might have problems with the name," I say.

"How come?"

"Well, my loser boyfriend was at the… errr… let me remember correct term now…" I say, staring ahead pensively and trying to recall the rather boring lawyer talk from a few weeks ago. "He said to me he'd been to some legal place. He was there yesterday. He filed a thing, I can't remember what it's called. But if I'm correct, I'm already legally Rose Petals in the music industry. Not that I want it that way…"

"Oh…" Suzie asks. "And why not?"

"I guess I wanted to be known as Tash," I say. "But he claimed it would be too boring for my supposed claim to fame to happen and topple, as he puts it, the 'queen of pop' off her pedestal."

"Hmm, if you and I pull off the scheme we could do something else funny," Suzie smirks with delight at me. "It could be an added layer of revenge…"

"In what way?" I ask.

"Rose Petals…" Suzie says curtly.

"Huh?"

"If I persuade him I'm better off as 'Rose Petal' as a stage name, then you and I get together with some ace lawyers, and make an agreement that because of the sameness of the names we either are a duo as Rose Petals OR that otherwise we can only ever be known by… Tash you said, right? Just Tash or something more?"

"Tash McKinsey," I blurt out. "McKinsey is my father's name. I want to show my mother that I care more about *his* opinion of me than hers…"

Chapter Three

"Ah right, and I'd then be Suzie B," she continues. "The 'B' stands for Braighton by the way. My birth name. So my added plan is, if you're okay with it, that the ONLY way either of us will Rose Petals is if you and I are a team and perform together. If neither of our boyfriends likes the idea with go to the lawyer and demand something that allows us to perform in a name WE want—"

"I'm cool with the idea..." I interject hastily. "Yeah, for definite..." I add a moment later.

+++

Twenty minutes later, Suzie and I are sitting opposite in a cosy cafeteria we found by chance, and we're comparing notes, so to speak, about how we ended up in each of our unfortunate situations of having a 'loser boyfriend.'

Because with the facts of the situation Mick was, and is, a loser. The more I'm talking with Suzie, who's quickly becoming a best friend, the more I realise deep down that I'm putting up with his kinks, his attitude issues, his idiotic outbursts of embarrassing me in the most annoying moments...

"So how long have you known him?" Suzie asks after sipping a few times from her drink.
"We're been serious for four years but I've known him for almost a decade," I reply. "It's... it's somewhat complicated..."

"Oh right. Whenever someone says that it always means they're not totally into the guy…" Suzie comments bluntly.

"Well, from where I sit I can assume your own relationship isn't all roses and butterflies," I snap angrily.

"I never said it was…" she whispers, looking down and fidgeting somewhat. She looks defeated by her own argument that had had the goal of finding out my fragile relationship status.

"I'll be frank with you. My relationship with Mick isn't as it should be…" I say hesitantly. "There are… there's something he does that make me wonder often whether he and I are meant be together…"

"In what way? I'm not trying to pry in personal stuff. Just trying out how similar we are…" Suzie comments. "We're more alike than either of us realised before…"

"I guess you're right…"

We sit silently for a good half hour before Suzie broaches the next topic of discussion. One a little more personal…

"I'm sorry if I offended you before…" she states firmly. "I didn't mean to be so… well, so hands on… so to speak."

I grin at her, and she blushes. It proves to me that she'd been as uncomfortable with the actions as I had been.

"So, not a lesbian?" I ask bluntly.

A quick head shake to confirm I'm right.

"Not bi I guess?" I ask next.

Another head shake.

"So, a straight girl chats up another straight girl for… what?" I ask, but now I speak without the earlier harshness in my voice, and I surprise myself with both the fact I even ask or that I almost sound sympathetic.

It's a side of my personality I hide. As they say… the reality of working in the music industry can be rather cutthroat at the best of times. Like all creative industries, apparently. Such as writing books like my sister is pursuing, or working in the movie industry as my childhood best friend seems to be embroiled in…

"What's your opinion of the music industry?" I ask.

"What do you mean by that? What does that got anything to do with our errand boyfriends?" Suzie counters my question with a very obvious question with a very obvious question of her own.

"Didn't you scream at him to turn on the mike…" I say flatly.

"Hmm, yeah, I did, didn't I?" Suzie answers.

"That's what I mean. WHO is in charge of your career, really?" I ask. "I know for definitely that Mick is trying to call the shots and dictate to me how I should sing, what I should sing, and with whom…"

"So it was his idea to go with Rose Petal then?" Suzie asks.

"No it was mine," I answer. "And it may be beneficial to you if you want to go along with my idea of how we can get our… revenge…"

"Revenge?" Suzie shrieks, then she laughs out loud. "You mean for them being two dick heads who want everything their way? I can live with that revenge…"

"Well, revenge for them being dick heads can come in many flavours," I suggest coldly. "One idea I now have is based on what you said in the restroom."

"You mean you want to go along with that idea…" Suzie says, smirking with delight. "I was kidding. And yes, I felt uncomfortable. But you were so convincing I believed I could pull off the plan I had."

"I had five years of acting classes…" I say. "And my first gig as an actress lands me in the middle of a porn movie as an extra. And yes, I had Mick to thank for that. Although it was a good thing. Bad choice, but still good. Because the 'fee' I received paid for all my music school lessons, so this here is my real first gig in a way where I'll be able to prove my worth as a singer…"

"And Rose Petals?"

"That was his idea, but I met with the lawyer a few days ahead. Used up the rest of the 'fee' to pay him to alter the contract somewhat," I answer. "There were five pages. Mick never saw the changes made to page four. All the rest is still as it was before except…"

I weigh up what to tell Suzie, and she guesses what happened by her suggestion, "… I will guess that a clause about the name Rose Petal was added," she suggests. "I will throw in a guess you made the contract more favourable for yourself somehow…"

I nod curtly.

"Smart girl…" Suzie blurts out. "But tell me what the 'change' entails?"

"It means that I can either use the name singular or plural," I answer. "I own the right either to be Rose Petal OR to be Rose Petals. I've been looking for a second person so it can be the latter option—When I heard you sing I decided I had to persuade you to—"

"You want me to team up with you?" Suzie asks. I note genuine surprise in her voice, and some genuine emotion I can relate to. It's the emotion of feeling worthwhile.

"You already said you had tried to get the name and failed," I continue. "I know I said earlier that I didn't enjoy using the name, but I've changed my mind. If you're interested, then WE can be Rose Petals. And screw Mick and... errr... I don't even know your boyfriend's name..."

"Timothy..." Suzie interjects. "Or, as I call him on a day such as this one when he can't do anything right—"

"Let me guess..." I interrupt Suzie, who nods encouragingly. "Fuck head?"

"That works," Suzie comments, smiling gleefully. I shrug at her. She guessed right...

+++

We're on our third bottle of cola when I do some good old Dutch courage and I pull out my notebook in which I write songs whenever Mick is out, or more precisely when he's going for job interviews. He's unemployed and thinks my singing career can set us up for a life of luxury...

I push the notebook towards Suzie, "I want to know what your opinion is of these songs I've been writing over the last few years. Tell me outright if they're a load of crap, okay."

Suzie pulls my notebook towards her and studies me. Obviously to determine my mood. Observing me obviously to assess whether I was just treating her like some fool, or really being serious. I catch a slight nod then she opens the notebook and her head bobbing shows she's trying to imagine the music that might play for the first song.

She smiles.

Another nod before she turns the page and seems to read the second song several times, then she looks up at me. I shrug and smile at her.

"Is this a song about Mick?" Suzie asks.

"No, it's about a guy I knew before I met him…" I reply. "His name is Tommy…"

"Seems like you still have feelings for him…" Suzie suggests. "I can hear it in your voice…"

"I guess so…" I mutter before sighing then add, "Yes, I do actually…"

"Did he ever know you can sing?" Suzie asks.

I shake my head and say, "We broke up a year before I tried to be a singer…"

"So if he sees YOU one day on television he might get a shock of his life," Suzie says.

I smirk and say, "I guess so…"

"Why did you break up with him?" Suzie asks, frowning somewhat.

"Actually, I don't know. We just stopped talking and then one day I was packing my bags to come to this city and never looked back," I explain. "We never argued or said anything to suggest we were breaking up."

"So he could sit somewhere and waiting for you to come back?" Suzie suggests.

"He might be married with kids by now for all I know. It's a decade ago…" I comment.

"Or he may not…" Suzie suggests. "Have you checked on Facebook for him?"

I shake my head and admits why not, "I don't have an account. Mick doesn't want me to be on it…"

"Ah, so your loser boyfriend is a control freak," Suzie says, laughing loudly now. "Anyway, I can check up on my account to see if he might be on it. If he is you have another purpose in life to make something of yourself and ditch the loser boyfriend. So his name is Tommy…?"

"Tommy Charlton," I reply without hesitation. I surprise myself once more.

"I think we must the revenge plan if ever you hook up with Tommy once again…" Suzie suggests. "And where does he live…?"

"In south London. Last I know, he had a job at a bank… Or at least that was the job he applied for…" I reply. "He's three years older than I am. I was born on the day they landed on the moon…"

"Okay, let me see what I can find. It might be tough though," Suzie says absentmindedly while she types on her cell phone. I crane my neck to see what she's typing. Obviously futile as the screen is in her direction…

I nod. Only cautiously because I'm uncertain what her objective is right now. For all I know she's got some souped up scheme planned out that will make me look like the fool I might be for trusting someone who pushes her hand down my panties. Part of me still feels the lingering aftereffect of being touched by her fingers…

"Did you find him yet?" I ask.

"Still looking…" she grunts. "It seems a common name."

"If you ever meet him, don't tell him that," I snort. "He always thought he had a unique name."

"Is his first name short for anything?" Suzie asks.

"His full name is—Let me think…" I say. "It's Thomas. Oh hang on, he said it was his second name…"

I stare at Suzie, defeated. It wouldn't be likely that a past love interest would list themselves on Facebook with a second name.

"WE will find him… okay," Suzie reassures me.

"You're doing more than I am," I say bluntly.

"Well, I guess I have to show you you can trust me…" Suzie says flatly. I stare at her and try to determine how honest she's with me right now. "You said he worked at a bank, right?"

I nod glumly, almost expecting her to say that none of the 'many people on Facebook' has a bank job.

"There are eight with the correct name… that being them listing as Tommy…" she continues. "… and two more listed as Thomas who all seem to either have a job at a bank OR who have had a job at one. What colour hair has he have?"

"Not sure. He dyed his hair jet black…" I reply.

"You never saw his pubic hair or the hair on his arms or legs? Didn't he have hair on his chest?" she continues, now sounding more like she's probing me like a suspect in a crime.

"Hmm, I can't recall seeing hair. I guess it's blond…" I suggest.

"I've eliminated all the people who may not be him, based on ethnicity," Suzie explains. "Or those who look too old. Your age…?"

"Almost twenty-three years old."

"Okay, that leaves us with sixteen possible people to check," Suzie says. "I can do it later when I'm home and can go on my computer. Then tomorrow I'll tell you what I found, and then we can make plans for after the concert about how we will find them, okay."

Chapter Four

After contemplating the suggestion for a few minutes, I nod curtly to show I understand the meaning of Suzie's words, though still feeling apprehension as to *why* a person I'd only met by chance will do so much for me.

But I guess it gives her a distraction from whatever is annoying her in terms of *her* boyfriend. I hadn't thought about Mick for the last thirty minutes…

"What if he's committed?" I ask.

"Then you have a reason to move on from him…" Suzie says, smiling. "Then you also know the answer of whether to stick with the current choice or totally move on and start a new phase of your life. And in case you wonder that's what I'm contemplating myself. I have to have a reason to call it quits on *my* loser boyfriend…"

I pull out my scarf from my bag when I open the outer door of the concert hall and the sharp, cold wind chills me to my bones. Checking my cell phone to determine if Mick ever bothered texting me, I glance over my shoulder at Suzie when I hear her speaking on her phone. I frown when I don't understand the language she's speaking…

I frown at her, feeling annoyed. Suzie sticks up a finger up to stop me speaking while she listens to someone speaking to her on her phone. At least, that's how I interpret it. I lift my arms to question her behaviour without speaking. She immediately places her finger to her lips and shakes her head. I feel deflated when I know what the answer will be when she hangs up.

Without knowing the language, I can tell by her body language that the news will not be positive or happy. I turn around, pull the scarf tighter and stare out over the square at the people walking over it.

"I just spoke with my friend who's a private investigator," Suzie's familiar voice rings out behind me. I turn and look at her, surprised. She continues explaining, "I asked her if there was a way to track down your boyfriend…"
"You mean she can find Tommy?"
Suzie nods once.
"How long might it take?"
"She said it can either take a few days or a few months," Suzie replies. "It depends on whether he wants to find him after all this time…"
"What if he doesn't?" I ask, now feeling some panic. "What then?"
"Then she will go for Plan B," Suzie says. "She gets people found. One way or another…"
"One way or another…" I echo, frowning momentarily when I realise that the result could easily be a dead end with me never finding Tommy again. I curse my stupidity for walking out on a guy nice to me and who'd care a lot about my wellbeing.

Definitely more than Mick ever did for certain, I think bitterly, *what a royal mess I made of my life really…*

"We'll make today, and also tomorrow until the auditions begin, the best days possible," Suzie comments reassuringly. "I think you should concentrate on that instead of Tommy. I'm certain my friend will do her magic and find him for you. She's got a track record to match it…"
"How many has she found so far?" I ask hesitantly.
"Over six-hundred people in the last decade alone…" Suzie answers, broadly smiling. "Do you remember the Amber alert about that little boy just a few months back…?"
I nod.

"She *found* the kid," Suzie continues. "They found him, starved from lack of food inside a silo of some sort, just a mile from his home. It's claimed he remembered his daddy mentioning something about water so had drunk from some dripping water all the time. He ate five massive burgers when they got him home…"

"How did your friend know where to find him…?"

"She remembered something from her own childhood. She grew up near where he went missing," Suzie explains. "She remembered that she and all her friends would play hide 'n seek near the silo. She decided that maybe this kid had done the same. Later it came out that he, his older brother and three of his brother's friends had been playing hide 'n seek near there. His brother spent most of the next four days helping to search for his brother after insisting it was his fault… Though apparently no one blamed him or his friends for what had happened…"

"So she'll find Tommy? Is that what you're suggesting?" I ask, and I notice the obvious scepticism present in my voice, to my annoyance.

"She'll find him. I told her to make it a priority," Suzie says, unfazed by my reluctance to believe her.

"And then what?" I ask.

"Then you go to him and at a minimum you make sure you and him are friends again," Suzie answers. "Please know that after this many years there's a chance—"

"I know what you're getting at… It's what I've already prepared myself for…" I interject forcefully. "I *know* he can easily be with someone else. If that's the case, I won't impede them…"

"And if he isn't?" Suzie asks. "What then? Are you going to dump Mick to get back with Tommy…?"

"I guess so…," I say after a few minutes contemplating the questions being fired at me.

"In the meantime, let's have a few days of fun and happy times. Let's get ready for the auditions," Suzie continues. "And also, let's do something about ridding us of two loser boyfriends. Okay?"

"If I didn't know better, it almost sounds like you got a thing against them…" I say. "But will your plan work?"

"I'm sure it will…" Suzie says. "Anyway, sit down. Show me your notebook with all those songs you've written and let me hear them…"

Suddenly, I feel happier because we're talking about something that I *care* about rather than Mick, and his idiot behaviour. I sit down opposite of Suzie and smile at her before I open my bag and pull out the two notebooks I use for song writing. I place them on the table between us. Suzie copies my actions, and she also pulls out a notebook from her own bag.

"I've been writing songs too but I know I'm not as good at it as you are if I base it on what you sung in the restroom," Suzie comments. "But if we will be in a band together, we might as well figure out which songs would work. I guess we need to make a list of song we'd do for an album—Are you sure about us becoming band members?"

"If there's anything I'm sure of, it's that," I say resolutely. "But I need to deal with the lawyer. I need to get the contract away from him and find a lawyer I can trust. He was the lawyer Mick had found for me so maybe Mick may try to influence him or manipulate him…"

"My friend knows a lot of lawyers…" Suzie comments.

"It needs to be a lawyer who knows about the entertainment industry though…" I counter. "It can't be a lawyer you pick from the phone book…"

"I guess that's the mistake I made. Which is why I ended up with all the mess of Timothy's efforts of sorting out legal stuff," Suzie continues, "I need a better lawyer myself—But let's talk about happier things… How did you come up with these songs?"

"I studied creative writing for two years, and one essay they assigned us was to write a poem," I explain, happy to talk about something different. "I also had been doing my acting and singing classes so wrote something I could perform in front of the class as a cappella. I knew if I could do it that way, it would work as a song for recording for an album later. You were singing a cappella earlier, did you realise that?"

"First time for everything…" Suzie says, grinning broadly. "I've sung nothing with no music before today…"

"You're good with it…" I comment. "My teacher suggested to me back then that if I could sing without music, I could perform anything whenever…"

"So, you studied music?" Suzie asks.

I nod affirmatively.

"I did similar—" Suzie continues. "Though, my parents weren't impressed with my career choice in the slightest. My mother wanted me to become an architect like her, and my father wanted me to go to business school... So, instead of complying with either of their wishes, I made my choice. Then one day, a few weeks after yet another argument with them, I just packed up my things and left home. I doubt I'll ever go back home..."

"Sounds terrible..." I say before sipping from the cola that the waitress placed on the table a minute earlier. "My story isn't is as terrible. My parents have always supported my choices of a career. My father paid for me to go to music school, and for my acting classes. My mother isn't as involved in my life as he is but she's fine with whatever I plan to do as long as I'm happy..."

"Are you happy? Are you really? Because of what you said before about Mick..." Suzie asks. "And, what about what happened regarding Tommy?"

"I guess not really," I answer after a pause.

"Because of how Mick behaves towards you...?"

"He's part of the problem, I guess," I answer defensively. "But, I'm discovering I made mistakes, and that I'm paying the price for those mistakes. I'm thinking I ain't no Cinderella who will find her Prince Charming. So, I make the best of life as it is..." I look down despondently and glance over the pages of my notebooks feeling some desperation. "I guess I'm trying to fix the mistakes..."

I glance up, annoyed when Suzie laughs loudly.

"What's so funny?" I ask coldly.

"It's something my friend said while I talked to her on the phone," Suzie explains. "She suggested there was a reason for you wanting to find Tommy. I'm guessing the real reason is that you feel lost..."

"I thought we would have fun," I snap. "Instead, you're making me feel worse and—"

"I'm so sorry..." Suzie breathes.

Suzie takes hold of my hand and gently squeezes it reassuringly, "It may sound like some cliche if I say it will be okay but it WILL be okay. I'm sure it will all be okay. It will be okay... all right?"

I nod curtly.

+++

We're both silent for the next twenty minutes then Suzie talks about happier topics, "Is this song some love song about Tommy…?"

I glance up and stare at her for several minutes, then I nod once.

It's the first time since I wrote the song I admitted the truth about the song. When I wrote it, Tommy had sat down beside me and asked about the song. At the time I wrote the song I told Tommy, it was just a random song. Of both of us, I'd been hesitant about admitting my feelings to him. He'd been telling me for months how he felt, even going as far as telling me he wanted to marry me. I had said no…

"I guess the biggest regret I have is saying no…" I mumble.
"No… No to what?"
It's one question I keep unanswered. But I'm guessing my face tells Suzie enough, and she smiles gently when I look up and stare at her again.
"I will not make promises but I'm certain that when YOU sing this song in our first televised performance, he'll come to find you," Suzie explains. "And that's if my friend has no luck in finding him first, but I know she'll be successful. She has a winning streak she's not willing to break…"
"So, I'm some bet?" I ask bluntly then I look down feeling embarrassed about the anger present in my voice.
"Not," Suzie answers quickly. "But I'm trying to make you feel happier. Or maybe I should go full on lesbian with you and get you in bed with me…"
I look up sharply, "What…? I thought you said you're not a lesbian…"
"I'm not, but I needed to say something to grab your attention from mulling over things you cannot change…" Suzie says, smirking slightly. "You look so glum we might as well find a funeral and go there instead of the auditions later on…"
"I'm sorry…" I say apologetically. "But Tommy is one topic I feel unhappy about even when I know I cannot change what happened between us. I did it to myself. I walked away from a perfectly good relationship for no reason. I guess I was scared about committing myself to a long-term relationship…"

Chapter Five

"I think the same goes for everyone..." Suzie says. "I think I'm the same with Timothy. But for entirely other reasons that I'll tell you about another day. Right now I want to concentrate on making the next few days the possible days for you so you can sing this song to the audition board with the happiness it deserves..."

"I'll do my best to get in a better mood..." I breathe.

"Well, if things go well, it should make both of us happy," Suzie says, squeezing my hand once more. "Concentrate on all that and let my friend and me concentrate on finding Tommy... Okay?"

I contemplate her words for several minutes, then I nod and say, "I guess I can't break her streak, can I...? I'll give her more information if that's needed to find Tommy. But I'll laugh so hard if he's in some place other than where I've been looking for him and where I end up picking up where we left off like no time has gone past..."

I guess we decided that the cafeteria was the wrong place for the fun we were both now looking for. So we went into town and go shopping and, as Suzie put it, "Damned with what the loser boyfriends think of us just abandoning them..."

+++

After Suzie repeats the words of disdain about our boyfriends for the fourth time, I make a suggestion she seems to like, "I doubt either of them even knows we're not coming back until the first auditions at five o'clock. Mick was told I would relax and exercise my vocal cords until then. He knows too well never to interrupt me when I'm exercising my vocal cords…"

"Timothy doesn't care at all what I do while I wait," Suzie comments. "He didn't even care about getting the settings for the microphone right when I was trying to sing earlier…"

"I think it will be funny as hell if they each think I'm you, and that you're me," I say, changing the subject back to what we'd been discussing in the restroom earlier in the day. "I doubt Mick will know the difference between us. We're similar heights and similar in how we act…"

"And we both like to be pleasured similarly…" Suzie groans. "I know I enjoyed it when you returned the favour. It still doesn't make us lesbians though. Sometimes girls just want to have fun in that way…"

"Yes, you're right…" I admit, but as I say the words, I feel shy and look down. "Although sometimes…"

"You mean to say you enjoy having sex with both?" Suzie asks.

"That's not what I'm saying. I just think it's fun to do it sometimes…" I answer.

Suzie stops walking, and after glancing around she pushes me against the wall. I feel her hand reach up under my skirt, then I gasp as her cold hand rubs my clit.

"So you like this…?" Suzie asks.

A moan escaping from my mouth is the only answer I can give her.

"Does Tommy know about this part of you?"

I shake my head.

"Would it matter if he knows?" Suzie asks next.

After a few moments of savouring her finger motions over my clit, I shake my head. But her next question has me gasping for air.

"Does he like threesomes with two girls? Or with three girls?" Suzie asks, smiling delightfully. These were questions I didn't expect and which I didn't know an answer for. So I stay silent, and then when I don't speak and even close my eyes, it's like Suzie changes her personality, "If we will do this later…" she says. "We need to be sure about you and me too, okay. I need to know how convincing you can be with orgasms…"

Suzie's finger flicks over my clit faster and I feel like my legs become jelly. I feel a rising heat between my legs as I become more turned on. Suddenly Suzie's weight against my body shifts and I feel her head lean against my pussy. She's kneeled on the ground in a narrow alleyway and licking my pussy in public. She sticks her tongue inside my pussy and the sensation it gives me has me grasping the brick wall behind me for support.

We hear sounds, and this causes Suzie to scramble to her feet. I stare at her in a daze for several seconds before we both giggle loudly.

"Now that was unplanned…" Suzie says calmly, beaming.

"What you did just down there, or the interruption just now?" I ask, glancing towards where the sounds had come from. I point at my skirt at the same time. "Was this planned?" I ask.

"Errr… no," Suzie whispers. "I guess it wasn't planned, but I enjoyed it…"

+++

After several minutes we walk on and turn right into the street filled with many shops and stop and stare around us with both of us trying to decide about where to go, "Come with me. I have an idea…" I say as an attempt to change topic, and for me to take control of what we will do next…

"What's planned?" Suzie asks.

"I saw a shop while I walked to the theatre from the train station. I wanted to visit it," I explain. "I think you'll like it too…"

"Lead the way…" Suzie says then pushes her arm through my arm with the intention for us to walk like we're sisters or something similar. Or, if the other thought occurring in my mind is correct, it's designed for people around us to think we're lesbians on the prowl. Deep down, the second option feels right. If I it inclined me otherwise Suzie might be the woman I'd go for. If I was a lesbian…

"It's over there," I say, pointing left. "I recognise the signage…"

"Okay, let's go."

We walk silently and briskly for the next five minutes until we reach the shop that had intrigued me so much the previous day when I arrived in this city. Suzie grins broadly when she stares into the shop.

"It's like a toy shop but with much old stuff inside…" Suzie comments, glancing up at me for a moment. "It reminds of The Nutcracker in a way…"

"You've seen the ballet?" I ask.

"Yeah, many times as a kid. Twice as an adult…" Suzie replies. "I might visit the theatre in the spring when they got another showing of it. Want me to book an extra two tickets in case my friend finds Tommy?"

"Who are you going with?" I ask.

"With my investigator friend. Her sister is Clara in this version of the ballet…" Suzie explains. "It's a more modern version of the ballet. It's why I will see it…"

"I'm intrigued now…" I say. "And if we find Tommy he'd likely go. One of the best memories I have of him is him taking me to see this ballet for my eighteenth birthday."

"Cool so then it's settled. I'll go to the website and add two extra tickets," Suzie says. "In the meantime, let's see what's for sale…"

I nod in response and we rush into the shop a moment later with both of us almost acting like two kids rather than two grown women.

We stare in awe around us, then at one another.

"Now we can have fun," Suzie suggests.

I nod in agreement.

"Good afternoon. How can I be of help?"

A man, perhaps as old as Clara's uncle in The Nutcracker, stands in a doorway at the back of the shop. He definitely could be in the ballet as the enigmatic Herr Drosselmeyer who gives Clara her nutcracker toy. I stare at the old man intrigued why he evokes such a powerful imagery and I'm certain that he knows this is the image any person coming to the shop may have of him. I nudge Suzie and when she glances at me her face has the same appearance, my face must show. It's almost like we'd stepped into another world when we walked into the shop…

"Can I help you with anything?"

"We visited this shop because it looks so intriguing," I reply. "Are these toys all handcrafted?"

"Yes, yes. I have my two sons who craft them for me, and my grandson also helps now…"

"I doubt he's going to be Tommy's grandfather before you get any ideas…" I whisper to Suzie, "Besides, I've met Tommy's grandfather…"

"Okay, I guess I can scrap that plan off my list, I guess," Suzie says with mock-sincerity. "But this place intrigues me…"

"We can look around and if we need help, we'll ask for it…" Suzie says loudly.

The old man nods, looks us over for a few moments, then turns and disappears into the room he'd come from moments earlier. Suzie and I look at one another when we hear him talking to someone.

"He's speaking in German…" Suzie whispers. "I learned German and Polish from my friend…"

"Was that what you spoke earlier?" I ask.

Suzie comments immediately, "My friend's husband is Polish. She learned the language from him, and she later taught me it. She and I speak the language to make sure we got more privacy…"

"Maybe you can teach me it too…" I suggest.

"It's a tough language to learn, but I can do that," Suzie says. "Especially if in the end we do create this band together as Rose Petals…"

"Yeah that's a deal then…" I say. "But we still need to fix the contract first before we do anything more about it…"

Suzie nods, then she prods my side and points to the shelf to our right. I turn to look and grin broadly.

"Okay, Suzie, so who of us will be Clara…" I ask. "Or shall we buy both of them so we both can pretend to be Clara and Louise? I wonder how much they cost…"

"They are sixty Euro each…"

Suzie and I both startle when a very young voice gives us the information we were so desperately trying to figure out. We turn at the same time. A teenager of maybe sixteen years old stands a few meters from us. He grins broadly at us both, then glances past us.

"The bigger ones on the bottom shelf cost ninety Euro each…" he says, providing us with further information before we ask for such information. "Grandfather asked me to make sure you were okay. He said that you probably would like to deal with someone younger than him…"

"He kind of reminded me of a person from a ballet…" Suzie blurts out.

"He gets that all the time. Even more so as he becomes older..." the boy says. "He likes it even when he doesn't show it. I also get the same treatment when the school girls all come to this shop. They all seem to think I'm Prince Charming or something ridiculous like that..."

"She thinks you're like Fritz," I say teasingly, pointing at Suzie. "She suggested to be Clara..."

"No, I didn't..." Suzie says defensively. "You suggested it..."

"I heard you outside the shop... You mumbled that with one of these I could pretend to be Clara..." I counter Suzie's comment. "So you're Clara, I'm Louise, and he can be Fritz..."

I nod at the shop owner's grandson.

"Almost right with the name. My name is Freddy... But, I can be Fritz if you want me to be that instead..."

All three of us grin at one another, then both Suzie and I eye the nutcracker toys. Suzie grabs one of the larger ones and as I don't want to be outdone I grab one of the other larger nutcracker toys. We both turn to our young host and grin at him teasingly.

"Now about the saying 'If you break it you pay for it'—" Suzie says. "If either of these get broken in any way we'll blame YOU... okay?"

"I promise not to break them..." Freddy says. "Is there anything else you want to purchase? We're closing in thirty minutes and are closed for a holiday until next week Sunday. We're visiting Grandfather's family in the country's south..."

"We put these on the counter then look around more. We'll call for you when we're finished..." Suzie says.

"There's a bell on the counter you can use to get my attention..."

After looking around the shop for another fifteen minutes, which causes us both to pick up a dozen or other items to buy, we walk to the counter and push the bell to get Freddy to arrive. He does so with his grandfather in tow. They smile at us pleasantly, even if the elder of the pair still makes me squeamish.

"That's three-hundred Euro for everything," Freddy says, looking up at his grandfather for approval. An approving nod from the old man confirms information is correct...

Chapter Six

Suzie stops me when I reach into my bag for my purse, "I'm paying for all this. This is my treat…" Suzie says softly.

I nod, and after a hesitation I lift my hand from my bag. Suzie pulls out her purse and places three-hundred Euro in notes in front of the old man, who nods approvingly, smiling an enigmatic smile now.

Just a few minutes later we stand outside the shop holding two large bags each. We stare at one another.

"Okay, did we want to buy all this stuff or did they just cause us to feel like we needed to do it?" Suzie asks. "I feel like they cheated us out of a lot more money than I wanted to spend even if we bought some rather interesting stuff…"

"To be honest, I'm uncertain," I comment. "But to meet someone who is so similar in his behaviour to the old man who gives Clara her nutcracker toy is rather interesting. It felt like we were in a different world in there. I don't think I will forget the experience in a hurry…"

Stepping into the street also means we're scrambling for cover as rain comes down ferociously within a minute. The day had started so pleasantly and sunny…

"Over there…" Suzie blurts out. She points across the street to a coffee shop. I nod and we rush across the street to the building; a two-storey building with a terrace. We rush inside then check that the contents of our bags had survived the onslaught from Mother Nature. A moment later we're sitting opposite of each other at one of the few unoccupied tables of the coffee shop. Most of the people who'd been walking along the street had the same idea as we did…

"Shall I get drinks and something to eat?" I ask.
"Sure…" Suzie replies. "Surprise me…" she adds as I walk off.
"I will…" I call out over my shoulder.

I walk to the counter where I'm greeted by a smiling waitress who glances past me for a moment then comments, "I guess the unexpected downpour caught you out. Need a towel to dry off your hair a bit? You're dripping everywhere…?"
"If it's not too much of a bother…" I answer.
"Wait, a moment. I'll get one. We have plenty in the backroom…"

I wait several minutes before the waitress is back with two towels that she hands to me, "One for your friend as well…"
"Thank you," I say, glancing back at Suzie who seems to busy herself with rescuing her sculpted makeup.
"How can I help you?"
"Oh, errr…" I say, then I look up at the notice board behind the waitress for suggestions of what to order. After a pause I speak again, "A pan pizza with pepperoni and onion, two colas and a plate of chips please…"
"Anything else?"
"No, thank you…"
"That's sixteen Euros…" the waitress says. "I'll bring over the food. You can help yourself from the fridge over there…"

I arrive a few moments later at the table with the cola and get a disappointed stare from Suzie.
"Is that it?" she asks.
"The rest is coming in a minute…" I counter.
"Oh okay. What did you get?"
"You told me to surprise you, so I will not tell you," I answer, laughing loudly when Suzie's face goes from somewhat annoyed to very.
"Yeah, yeah, I said that, didn't I…?"

"You did…"

Suzie glances outside where the rain is still coming down so hard that it creates tiny streams of river along the street.

"I guess the weather puts a dampener on the rest of our plans of fun…" Suzie comments. "I guess that we can't go shopping now… oh well…"

We both glance up as the waitress arrives just then with our order.

"Pizza?" Suzie comments. "And chips… You know how to make a girl happy. And the pizza comes complete with my favourite toppings…"

"So I'm forgiven for not saying what I had ordered?"

"You are…"

"I couldn't stop overhearing but if you're after shopping, we have a back entrance in this coffee shop that exits out into the shopping centre…" the waitress interjects. "Which is all dry and warm…"

Both Suzie and I stare surprised at the waitress with each of showing a happy broad grin on our face, like she has just told us we'd just won the lottery.

We stare at one another, we both giggle, then we say "We can go shopping…"

"Thank you," Suzie says to the waitress.

"You're welcome…" the waitress says before walking away.

After a moment of staring at one another Suzie and I each grab one piece of pizza and we devour it silently, followed quickly by similar actions with all the remaining food.

After finishing all the food, Suzie and I get up quietly, wave goodbye to the waitress and rush towards the doorway she points towards. We find ourselves in a wide, bright shopping centre that could easily be the advert for this city to attract tourists and shoppers to visit…

+++

We've visited five shops when Suzie looks at her phone and makes us both realise that our fun time at the shopping centre has come to an unexpected end for now. Now we have to get back to the theatre on time with eleven heavy bags.

"Let's get a taxi…" I suggest when I look through the doors of the shopping centre. It's raining even harder than when we had gone into the coffee shop.

"Good idea…" Suzie says. "And just so you know… I'm rather bemused about why the loser boyfriends haven't bothered to find out where either of us is. Have you've had any texts from Mick at all? I have had none from Timothy all day long since I left him alone with his crap…"

"Not had any text from him…" I say. "I've texted him several times asking what he's doing. No texts back from him at all…"

"I guess that behaviour proves that he doesn't really care," Suzie suggests. "Not really, huh… Same as my loser boyfriend. I'm thinking I will be better off single for the rest of my life, and by virtue I should have listened to a friend from my school days. She always said she didn't want a relationship or anything. And said there wasn't anything wrong about living in that way…"

"Wise advice, but some of us want to be with someone…" I say.

"Yeah, yeah, I know. You can try to get a relationship going with Tommy, but for me at least, for now at least, the dating days are over," Suzie says. "Single life appeals to me after the way Timothy has behaved. And I know I might meet someone new…"

"Just take your time for some time alone, okay. Or more precisely, give yourself time for yourself," I say, holding Suzie's hand. "And do you know we sound like a pair of advice columnists right now…"

Suzie chuckles at my suggestion, adding her own assessment, "Maybe a career choice if we're too old to be singers and—"

Suzie stops speaking when a taxi screeches to a halt a few yards from where we're waiting.

+++

The taxi driver stares at us. I notice it and nudge Suzie. I glance sidelong at her and see her nod. When I stare back at the taxi driver, his gaze changes from just plain curiosity to lusting. I bet he wishes he could convince us to go home with him…

"Do you know the theatre?"

I snap out of my gaze and stare at Suzie incredulously. She sounded so rude just then. I glance sidelong towards the taxi driver, who now seems to look in all directions but ours. I guess Suzie snapped him out of lusting after two women in their twenties who'd stepped into his taxi. He nods plainly, glances over his shoulder to determine the traffic's status and he's off. His pursuit to deliver us as speedily to our destination reminds me of the scene where Harry and Ron are in a car in a certain movie that I'd care to forget I ever went to see; mostly because of all viewings I could have chosen, I'd ended up there with five hundred school kids staring at the only other adult there and the eight irate teachers sitting on benches at the side wall didn't count.

"You can slow down..." Suzie snaps angrily when a pothole has her jostled again me. I grunt a swear word under my breath. And another one when the taxi screeches to an abrupt halt.

I look outside the taxi. I'm confused.

"This isn't..." I begin to protest but Suzie stops me speaking with an urgent prodding into my ribs, "... this is the perfect place to let us out. How much?" Suzie interjects, directing the question towards the taxi driver.
I stay silent...

The whole taxi journey took just fifteen minutes. We both stare after the taxicab as it drives off fast and then turns a corner. We glance at one another then a moment later we're both leaning against one another laughing hysterically. I can see people walking past who are staring at us with odd expressions wondering what the hell is wrong with us...

"What was all that about?" I ask between a few snorts of a giggle.
"Didn't you see how he was looking at us...?" Suzie counters. "I think he might have tried to chat us up if I wasn't so rude on purpose..."
"I saw him staring at us..."

"I'm guessing he's some dodgy taxi driver who tries to chat up every female passenger that he picks up," Suzie explains coldly. "But that said, I saw him chat up an unfortunate woman on the day I arrived in the city. She slapped him because of how he was behaving towards her…"

"You mean to say we were in a taxi with some creep…?"

"To be honest, I don't know, but I wasn't comfortable with him staring at us all the time…" Suzie continues. "But that's not why we ended up here. Beside the concert hall there's this older theatre. He might have thought we meant this place when I asked him to take us to the theatre. The concert hall is on the other side, and we can be there in under ten minutes. In the meantime, let me show you why I brought you here…"

Suzie has my curiosity on full alert now. I guess the fun can begin in all honesty…

Once we've evened out the load of the bags, we carry with us - and now I wonder if that was the real reason the taxi driver was curious, we're somewhat backtracking along the road we'd arrived in. While we walk Suzie decides to explain how she knows of this theatre.

"My father took me to this city over a decade ago when I was a teenager. He works in art financing, or more precisely he did when I came to the city with him," Suzie explains. "There used to be a restaurant just over there…"

Suzie lifts her left arm laden with bags and attempts to point, but a moment later she places her bags on the ground and points, "… the red-bricked building with white gables…"

"It's a pretty…" I say. "What happened to the restaurant…?"

"I heard they went out of business about four years ago…" Suzie answers. "Something happened, and it caused a scandal, and a month afterwards the restaurant was closed."

"The food was that bad?" I venture a guess to the cause of the demise. "Or something else?"

"It had something to do with the wife of the owner having an affair…" Suzie answers. "The owner found them in the kitchen making out on top of the range. He'd fucked her so hard she'd pissed all over it. Then a week later several people got ill eating their cooked food—You wanted to explore being private detectives. Here's your chance…"

"Now you have me curious…"

Silently we cross the street and when we arrive at the old restaurant, we can hear sounds coming from inside. We stare at one another for a moment, "It doesn't look like they should occupy it," Suzie comments. "But someone's playing music inside…" Suzie leans against the nearest boarded-up window, then shakes her head. "I can hear music but that's about it…"

I copy Suzie's actions and listen against the window, then I glance at Suzie, "Should we check it out?"

Suzie shrugs her shoulders and is silent for several minutes.

"Should we?" I ask again.

"I'm curious too," Suzie blurts out. "This building apparently has, so many stories attached to it…"

Suzie opens her bag and pulls out a booklet and hands it to me. I open it and glance through its pages. At page thirty I stop, read a moment, then glance up at Suzie.

"This is about the scandal you just mentioned…"

Chapter Seven

Suzie nods and gives me her own assessment, and she makes it obvious she's read the whole booklet, "The building was built in the late nineteenth century. In the thirties, it was a speakeasy. Maybe one of few of them outside the USA."

"I read something about how they started for my history classes when I was still in school…" I comment. "It started originally as a place where smugglers would meet in Britain. A memoir from the nineteenth century mentioned it. I guess it fits in with the sordid history of this place based on what's being talked about in this booklet…"

"That's why this place fascinates me so much," Suzie says. "But the biggest mystery right now is who might use an empty building."

"Modern day smugglers perhaps…" I suggest.

"Check out page eighteen…" Suzie says.

I nod once, and I comply with her suggestion for what to read next in this fascinating booklet. After a few minutes, I look up at Suzie and ask her, "What's so interesting about this? Or more precisely, what's so interesting about it to you?"

"When I was reading your songs, the one called Pretty In Blue, it reminded me of this building. Check the next page…"

I turn the page and I gasp…

The woman in the photo stands in an alluring pose beside a piano could easily be my grandmother…

What I hadn't told Suzie 'yet' is that my *Pretty In Blue* song is based on a story that my father told me many times throughout my

life about my grandmother. She'd apparently worked as a 'moll'…
One reason I'd come to this city is the curiosity about my father's
family. She could have easily worked as a moll in a place such as this
restaurant. And now at least a part of my father's story, and a few of
the words in my song, match the appearance of the woman in this
hundred-year-old photo. I lift the booklet closer, and I squint my
eyes to check if this photo might be… my grandmother…

"Is she familiar to you for any reason?" Suzie asks. I glance up
and she's craning her neck to glance at the page at the same as I am
doing it.

"If I didn't know better, this photo could be of someone that my
father told me about…" I say.

"Who?" Suzie asks.

"My grandmother. She had a job as a moll in this city…" I reply.

"What is a moll…?"

"Well, I guess we'd call them sex workers these days…" I say,
grinning now as I was discussing a story that had me enthralled
whenever my father told me it.

"You mean this could be your grandmother?" Suzie says,
grabbing the booklet from my hands and studying the woman
carefully. "If I didn't know better, the song you wrote describes this
woman. Complete with blue muffs—Unless the colours have been
added later on."

I grab the booklet from Suzie and study the photo, then I point
below the photo, "It says this is a colour photo from the thirties. The
earliest colour photos have existed since the second half of the
nineteenth."

"So it could be her…? Or someone similar…" Suzie suggests.
"The words from your song tell of the woman with her blue muffs
who was in love with the piano player, a love forbidden by the norms
of the time. What happened to your grandmother? Do you know?"

"I only know what my father told me, and what he was told by
my grandmother and her sister…" I answer. "It's a story that's
fascinated for most of my life…"

"So, why the use of this word… errr… a moll," Suzie asks.

"She referred to it in that way according to my father," I reply.
"From research I've discovered it's an old-fashioned word. She'd be
referenced as a sex worker these days as I said before."

We're both distracted when the music inside the building

changes to fast-paced jazz, "Who the fuck listens to that music?" Suzie asks, frowning with clear annoyance present in her voice.

"Maybe tell them to shut it up…" I say teasingly. "But I want to point out that my grandmother was a jazz singer. She was that too…"

"Sorry…" Suzie says apologetically. "I honestly didn't know…"

"You couldn't have…" I suggest and take hold of Suzie's hand. "But seriously, shall we go inside or at least try to see what's going on…?"

"Sure…"

+++

Fifteen minutes later, we've finally found the entrance to the old restaurant. It's not at the front of the building. It worries me for us to have to walk through narrow alleyways to get to the 'entrance' at the back…

"Can you still hear the music?" I whisper to Suzie, nudging her to stop her from walking off unnecessarily.

"I think it's coming from upstairs. Shall we check it out or do you want to go…?" Suzie asks.

"I'm too curious to go," I whisper.

I hold up the booklet and point at the wall behind the woman in the photo, "My father told me that my grandmother had told about this painting. That makes me think this is where she was a singer… well, and a moll, too," I reply. "But how did you ever find this book, or this place in the first place?"

"Actually, that's the silly part of it all. Timothy was sent out to get some 'entertaining reading' for me three days ago, and besides the few magazines he bought me, he also bought me this booklet. At first, I was annoyed for him bringing me reading material that was not my usual reading material, but when he went to a bar last night I stayed at the hotel instead. I picked up this booklet, read it from cover to cover…" Suzie explains. "I came here yesterday to check this place out, but I didn't feel okay going inside on my own…"

"And we're safe now, right?" I say sarcastically. "Do you plan on bashing any potential adversaries upstairs with all these bags?"

I hold up my five bags filled with our shopping efforts up in front of my face for several seconds before the strain in my muscles causes me to drop my arm again. I grunt as pain shoots through my upper arm a moment later…

+++

We stop halfway on the stairway when the stairs creak loudly stops us in our tracks. We stare at one another, then we both giggle like schoolgirls. After a few minutes, we find the courage to walk on…

"We should have gone for a stronger drink first for some Dutch courage…" Suzie whispers.

"We could go do that and come back later…" I suggest. I hope my voice doesn't betray how scared I feel, really.

"No, let's keep going on," Suzie says. "Don't you want to check out if the room in the photo is still there…?"

Suzie glances at me questioningly. After a few moments thinking I nod.

"How much do you know of the room where your grandmother performed?" Suzie asks.

"My father told me how she described it to him…" I reply. "Last time he talked about it I wrote it down. It's from those notes I wrote the song."

"So we go on?"

I nod affirmatively.

+++

Tension between us is palatable once we glance around the corner into the room. Once we discover it empty, we glance at each other and nod, smiling broadly. We step into the room and glance around…

"This isn't the room…" I mumble.

"Okay, let's check the next room…" Suzie whispers.

"We don't have much time left before we have to be back," I counter. "Maybe we should come back another day…"

"Okay, five more minutes and then we'll go. This place creeps me out…" Suzie says.

"I don't feel happy being here," I suggest. "I don't believe in haunted houses but this place…"

"Best not to read other parts of that book then…" Suzie says, laughing loudly.

"Are you saying this place is haunted?" I ask.

"Some people say it is haunted…" Suzie suggests. "Because of certain things that have happened here. Like the murder of the mistress of the first owner. They found her in bed with a guy who supposedly she had an affair with at the same time. The owner killed them both in the bed. After that happened, this place would have many mishaps for anyone who owned this building…"

"Hmm, something of that corresponds to something my grandmother told my father. It's apparently one reason she quit her job here and left the city," I explain. "That's the connection I have with this city. She was born in this city. She moved, and soon afterwards met my father's father. They married six months later and a few years later, after the war, my father was born…"

"That sounds interesting…" Suzie comments. "So, if she's the person in the photo, it's of her before she left her employment here. That leaves the mystery of what she saw happen here and how it affected her…"

"I would search for the source of the story while I was here, but now I'm glad I met you by chance," I admit. "It saved me many hours or days of searching."

We walk on to the next room and realise now that the music we were hearing is likely coming from the neighbouring building. We stand near the parting wall and the music has the same muffled sound to it as below when we leaned against the boarded-up window. This would mean the building is empty.

Suzie and I stare at one another and it's clear we both feel and appear deflated.

"Let's just look around then we'll leave, okay…"

+++

It's ten minutes later when we enter a room that I recognise immediately. I pull the booklet from my bag where I'd placed it for ease, and I look again at the photo of the unknown woman, and then look at each wall.

"This wall…" I comment, pointing to the wall on my right. "The piano would have stood over there. And the lighter area on the wall is where the painting was…"

I step forward and position myself, glancing back to judge distance, then I say, "This is where she stood…"

"Give me the booklet for a moment..." Suzie says, reaching out for the booklet. I hand the booklet to her. She steps backward a few paces, then seems to study me. "Stand in the same posture as her. I might see if there are similarities between you. Because that may make it more likely that this is your grandmother..."

I comply and try to stand 'sultry' leaning against an imaginary grand piano. After a few minutes of silence, Suzie pulls out her cell phone and takes a photo, "That's just in case," she says. "We can put this photo and the photo of you and her side by side in some photo editing software I've used before..."

"How can it help us?" I ask.

"It can compare facial features between you and the woman in the photo," Suzie explains. "We can just compare the room visually but facial features is trickier..."

"And if it suggests there are similarities?" I ask sceptically.

"Then you can search out more of the history of this building..." Suzie replies. "Hence why I said that this can be the start of a career as a private investigator. You already confirmed that part of the evidence squares up with what you were told of your family's history. If we discover more, it will help you even more..."

"I didn't tell you yet the reason I chose 'Rose Petals' as the name for the band..." I say, smiling conspiratorially at Suzie. "There are several reasons. One of them being the story about my grandmother. I said she was a moll. Her name as a moll was, and don't laugh please, well, she called herself Rose Petals according to my father. He said she was very proud of the name. Her name was Rose. My grandfather was Pete McKinsey so according to my father she saw it as serendipitous, as he always put it, when he met her by chance..."

"Oh really, so I guess us meeting is as serendipitous," Suzie say, grinning then she glances at her cell phone and her facial expression changes to shock, "Oh no, let's go. We will be late otherwise..."

We rush through the door, only stopping occasionally to capture as many features of the various rooms we pass through on each of our cell phones as quickly as we can even if I'm convinced that most of them will just be a blurry mess and not useful.

"Tash, we can go this way—" Suzie says, and she pulls me to the right rather back-tracking us back to the road we came from earlier. "It's a shortcut back to the concert hall. I discovered it by chance when I was here the last time..."

Chapter Eight

I glance into the alley and frown a moment then sigh and blurt out, "Lead the way. I'm already lost…" then I breathe a few times before adding, "I can't wait until I can sit down and relax…"

"We can put the bags in a cabinet I rent in the concert hall. I put stuff there that I don't want Timothy to see," Suzie whispers when we stop to catch our breath a moment.

"So you can go on shopping sprees like we did today?" I ask, grinning.

Suzie nods then she blushes which tells me that the answer is affirmative even if she will not answer me. After a few minutes she answers me, "I enjoy shopping, but Timothy says I spend way too much money on it. But it's spare money of money I've earned, I've been paying most of the bills for the last five years…"

"To me that sounds like he's controlling you in other ways that are not so nice," I hiss. "If that's another reason for what you said about wanting to leave him, I can understand the reasons now…"

"Everyone always says that a guy acting like the bad guy is okay and acceptable but personally I don't think that's okay at all," Suzie says, looking down now and losing most of her outward confidence for a moment. "I guess that's the other reason I'm fed up with him…"

"If that's the real reason you dreamt up the act of revenge, with us swapping boyfriends, then count me in," I say, frowning angrily. Now I knew the real reason for Suzie's behaviour all day long I wanted to help her…

Almost two hours later we're sitting side by side in the corner of a room that the organisers have designated as a 'green room.' As I'm bored with waiting for my turn to audition, I use the time to check constantly my cell phone for messages from Mick knowing that he'd been alone upstairs for several hours now. And not bothered about where I am or what I'm doing right now…

"So, about our plan…?" I begin my conversation with Suzie. She jerks like I just scared her with my words.

"Hush about it," Suzie hisses. "Too many people here right now. We can talk after they've all left…"

"Well, it was about our plan for a band, but okay…" I grunt.

"We can talk about that plan, but still I'd be careful," Suzie says. "If you say the wrong thing and someone hears it, they can steal ideas from us. Until we have a contract with 'someone' we're not protected from people stealing ideas. It happens all the time apparently…"

"So maybe I shouldn't have shown you my songs until we signed a contract…" I grunt again.

"Oddly you're okay, really. You said you went to this lawyer person and did some contract," Suzie says. "But that only protects you for now. I'd say you need to find yourself—or us—a better lawyer if you want your boyfriend out of the picture. Same goes for me, really. The interfering 'prick' can ruin all our chances to make it big with the two of us…"

I laugh loudly at the comment, even if I meant it as a serious remark. I get a snort from Suzie in response, "I can see the funny side of it when I analyse what I just said from your perspective."

"The reason I just had to laugh just now is because the opposite is true and I made provision in the contract. I got them to add a paragraph to it that states that I can seek one or more band members of my choice, and until both the new band member and I had signed a contract together that meets both our approval that all my songs belong completely to me," I say, grinning broadly the moment Suzie stares at me incredulously. "Also, until next year copyright protects the Pretty In Blue song. That's when the seventy years ends since my grandmother died. She left her music and songs as a legacy to any children my father would have. He had just one child interested in a singing career… me. So next year in accordance to her wishes and other legal stuff that my father checked was all valid and such the songs become all mine. I show you songs that were her songs, so law already protects most of the songs. That's why I know I can sing any of them at this audition without the risk of anyone copying them or stealing them or whatever…"

"Smart grandmother, smart Rose…" Suzie says, beaming. "So I guess you're doing things in a similar which makes *you* as smart."

"I guess so," I comment. "But the legal stuff is a hotbed, and if you do things in the wrong way, you can get in some serious problems. Both legally and financially from what I've found out so far of the subject. I did classes at college about entertainment law, but I'm no expert. My father knows about contracts because of his former job for a big company he worked for, but he said the legal stuff for the entertainment industry differs from what he knows. He told me to find a lawyer I can trust who knows all this stuff before I sign if they accept me at these auditions…"

"I think he's right," Suzie says. "Look at the mess Timothy got in trying to create Rose Petals as my performance name when you already own it. And no, I'm not after the name. After hearing about your grandmother I now understand fully that the name belongs to you… It belongs to your family, mostly to you because of the legacy pledge she did. You *should* honour your grandmother. Why don't you sign 'Pretty In Blue' at the auditions? I'm certain you'd secure the contract with them based on just this song alone."

"I can lend you one of my other songs as audition material seeing as you're going to BE my band mate," I suggest.

"No, I think I'll sing the song I was singing in the restroom," Suzie counters. "I want to see Timothy's face when I sing it. He hates the song, or so he says…"

"He's an idiot if he hates the song…" I comment.

"He's definitely an idiot…" Suzie says. "I'll be glad when I'm rid of him…"

"So, about our 'other' plan?" I say gleefully. When Suzie gives me an annoyed stare, I plainly smile at her, then give her a playful wink. She frowns, but when I stay silent Suzie realises that I'm just teasing her a bit. My eyes dart sideways, and she realises I remember not to speak about those plans when people are still present. She leans closer and whispers, "I think those six girls are together so once they've gone we talk, okay…"

I nod once, then observe the girls for their efforts to prepare for the upcoming auditions. Okay, the first round isn't really the auditions but more a rehearsal for the auditions so everyone knows what to do. I cringe when one girl is tone deaf in her execution of what's supposed to be a chorus. Suzie snorts under her breath and whispers, "That won't get her a place in the line-up…"

"I agree, but I guess people have to start somewhere… somehow…" I whisper back.

"Maybe like we did with music lessons and singing lessons," Suzie says under her breath. "I think she'll be heartbroken when it's a no…"

"Rejection comes with the territory," I comment. "I can't even count the number of rejections I've had so far just this year alone and I've been doing this for a decade or longer…"

"And no one gave you a record deal yet in that time?" Suzie asks.

"I was in a band for five years before I met Mick and earning good from singing other people's songs," I answer.

"What happened to the band?"

"Mick happened oddly…" I reply. "But the band was already falling apart, anyway. The two guys who started the band started arguing about music they wanted to play. Then Mick got involved, caused an argument and within a week the band was no more…"

"So it's Mick's fault you have no record deal?" Suzie asks.

"Yes…" I reply. "But there's more to the story and it would take me hours to explain and I rather do it when I know that Mick is out of the picture. If he walked in while I was telling it he could end up causing headaches for me, for us, that will haunt us from now all the way to when I'm on my deathbed decades from now…"

"It's that bad…?"

"It is… The lead singer of the band might sue me personally if he knew that Mick and I are still together," I reply. "I guess I've got my own sordid story of abusive behaviour I want to get out of my life for good. So without going into details until we're alone, I've been thinking things over and yes, I want to go along with the plan you have. Have you done acting classes too?"

Suzie nods affirmatively.

"Then it's settled. When we do 'it' we'll use every ounce of our acting skills to persuade them they're—" I lean closer to Suzie and hiss conspiratorially the remaining words, "… to see if they know they're not fucking their own girlfriends…"

"Shh, before they hear you…" Suzie hisses.

"Yeah, I know. That's all I'll say. But I was here for an entertaining day filled with fun," I continue. "So far it's been an excellent day of fun but now I want THAT also to be fun for us…"

We both glance over towards the group of girls and I grin at the youngest of them when our eyes lock. I guess in her mind we're just arguing about the upcoming auditions. I feel sorry for her because she looks like she doesn't even want to be here…

+++

Suzie and I glance at one another when the group of girls leave the room, with the youngest of them giving me a shy hand wave as she leaves trailing her companions. I wave back, and glancing sideways I see Suzie waving too then blowing a kiss towards the girl. The girls smiles shyly at us and then is gone.

"Can we talk now?" I ask.

"Yes, now we can talk…" Suzie says. "Without these passes they cannot come down here." Suzie holds up the badge pinned to the upper part of her cardigan then continues, "We had to wait because those girls could say something about it, they heard us talk about sex and all that stuff…"

"Yeah, I understand that. So, what's the plan?" I say, repeating the earlier question asked. I smile at Suzie when she glances at me again.

"I checked out the rafters… well, the top floor or whatever they call it," Suzie explains. "On the way up there's a corridor with two rooms either end and stairway to a lower floor. I thought it's out of the way enough so we could execute the plan there. It's a just case of getting the guys there with no protest…"

"I guess we both have the same idea for exploration as I've been up there too," I say. "I visited it this morning. I already convinced Mick we could have sex there with no one seeing us. He and I visited the left room early this morning…"

"That means that half the problem has been solved…" Suzie

comments. "Now for my sordid problem to be solved…"

Suzie laughs when I gape at her. She already sounds like someone who'd all but given up on her relationship with her boyfriend. But remembering what she'd said earlier, I don't blame her in the slightest for starting 'let go' in her mind.

"So, you're certain of wanting single life then?" I ask.

Suzie nods then says, "I think I've read way too many romance novels over the years where always the guy is some nasty piece of work who treats the girl badly and she still loves him unconditionally. I'm realising now that's the wrong relationship to have with any person. I think someone needs to come up with a story where the good guy gets the girl…"

"I guess that's why you seem to root for me to find Tommy…" I breathe, looking down a moment and flicking my thumbs against one another aimlessly.

"Tommy sounds like a decent guy to be honest. Not someone to walk away from," Suzie says. "But I guess we make mistakes and yours is not realising he was a good catch until you'd upped and left. I'm really hoping my friend finds him and then that he wants you back. I really hope he's still single and looking for YOU and has done so for all these past years…"

Chapter Nine

Looking back up at Suzie I smile weakly then I tell her, "I hope so too. I really miss him now. I should never have left him. He and I could have been married by now. I was…errr…I was scared of the idea of getting married at the time. I saw what happened to the marriage of my parents. I was badly affected by it…"

I wipe away a tear that trickled from my eye before I continue talking, "If he's found I want you to get your friend to confirm first if he's single still," I mumble. "If he's married, I don't want him to know I was searching for him. I don't want to impede any existing relationship he might have now."

Suzie places an arm around my shoulders and squeezes encouragingly, "I'll text my friend now and tell her to be aware of this wish, okay. If she finds him and he's single, I'll get her to text me back she found him and he's available for you to get things mended with him…"

"Thank you."

I watch as Suzie's fingers nimbly type out a message; obviously in Polish as she'd mentioned learning it from her friend.

A moment later, a reply flashes up on the screen. Suzie glances up, and she smiles briefly at me, whispering, "She understands. She'll comply with your wishes. She says she may already have some positive leads…"

"So she might find him faster than I thought then?" I ask.

"She could have him found before the end of this week…" Suzie says, grinning now. "Oh boy, I'm getting excited about this now. It's good when a love story has a happy ending…"

We lean in so we can talk about the 'other stuff' without the possibility of accidentally being overheard by anyone, least of all either boyfriend if they disobeyed the rules and search us out. The rules of the audition mean that only the performers can be in the green room waiting for the call from the director in charge of the auditions.

We constantly glance towards the door whenever we hear footsteps beyond it, and we wait before continuing to talk until they've faded away. We're suddenly interrupted by each of our phones buzzing, and after quickly checking them, it's suddenly clear that the boyfriends are now aware we've been missing.

"Dammit…" I mutter. "Now he realises something has gone me for hours. He wants to meet with me…"

"Right now?" Suzie asks. "Tell him you're supposed to wait here…"

"He's at the top of the stairs in the corridor," I grunt. "I guess he'll barge in here and cause me headaches if I don't talk with him quickly…"

I get up and walk to the door. As I exit the room, I hear Suzie's comment, "He's a control freak, don't you realise that…"

Just outside the green room after closing the door, I pause a moment. I realise Suzie is right. So damned right…

+++

Minutes later I'm glaring at Mick who smiles at me with his annoying condescending smile. For once I don't smile back…

"What in the fuck do you want?" I snap at him.

"I wanted to know if you were hungry and want me to get food…" Mick says, ignoring my anger.

"I've eaten already..."

"Oh, when? And without me?" Mick asks coldly.

"You don't dictate what I can do or when," I say, remembering what I'd said hours earlier to Suzie. My stance softens then, and I lure Mick to the room upstairs near the rafters, "... but if you WAIT, I'll make it up to you later. I was exploring this building a bit. There's a quiet room where no one would find us..."

I hold my breath as I wait for Mick's response. Would he believe me? Will he leave me alone until later...?

I move closer to Mick and press my body against his. He reacts to my actions, but I ignore them mostly, repeating my earlier words, "There's a quiet room we can use later..."

Mick grins playfully. He realises now, finally, what I'm implying with my suggestion.

"But first I need to do this audition, okay?" I continue. "I may get called. They cannot see you here and if I'm not in THAT room I will miss my spot..."

I point towards the door of the green room.

"The rules forbid any person who isn't an artist from being there," I continue. "The previous artists were some kids who sat there without their parents. I felt sorry for them..."

"Who the fuck allows their kids be alone in that way?" Mick grunts.

"I guess the organisers do," I answer. "I guess the parents are in the audience. They left the green room just over five minutes ago. It means they've had their call fifteen minutes before they go on. The youngest of them almost looked like she'd burst out in tears..."

I know I'm now just playing Mick for a fool and trying to get him to feel a sympathy of any kind.

It seems to work based on his next comment.

"I'll go sit down in the audience then. To make sure those kids are okay," Mick says. "But can we go to the room you mentioned after you're done with your audition?"

"It's a promise..."

I watch Mick walk off. At first he's reluctant to go, but then I entice him in the *usual* way to cause a certain well-known reaction from him. He grins at my naked boobs when he glances back at me. A moment more and he's gone…

I turn and re-enter the green room where Suzie sits waits, anxious and impatient. I smile at her, then flash my boobs at her too. She gapes in response.

"It's sorted…" I say, smiling conspiratorially.

"What's sorted?" Suzie asks.

"Well… the thing," I answer. "I've convinced him we could go upstairs for some—" I stop speaking. I open the door momentarily and I glance in each direction in the corridor then close it again, "… I convinced him I want to have sex with him there…"

"Oh wow, I didn't realise all this would be this easy," Suzie blurts out before she laughs loudly and uncontrollably, flopping sideways on the bench she's occupying now. I laugh too because for the first time in years I feel in control of my destiny and my own desires.

"So you're certain that Timothy will go along?" I ask.

"I just talked with him and he'll meet me after the auditions, similarly to you meeting Mick," Suzie says, breathing deeply to calm herself.

We stop speaking another time when footsteps pass the door.

"Those people walking past the door freak me out," Suzie whispers. "My heart jumps every time…"

"The same for me…" I say. "The longer we're waiting, the more nervous I get. I guess that's the reason for this room, too. To allow performers to be settled before they perform…"

"You weren't as nervous before you spoke with Mick just now," Suzie comments. "Now you look like you'd tear this room apart…"

I sit down abruptly.

Deflated.

Defeated by Suzie's logic.

I look at the floor, feeling pensive now.

"It will be tougher to pull all this off if you're not in the right mindset. Pull yourself together. Pretend it's an audition for a movie or something like that," Suzie breathes. "Remember that you need to be in the right mindset for your audition…"

I breathe in deeply and look up at Suzie with a frown plastered on my face.

"I guess what I said to you about the boyfriend being too controlling applies to myself," I mumble. "I think I realised how controlling he is when I was just talking to him…"

"What did he do? Or more precisely, what did he do to you?"

"It's not what he did, but more the lack of showing he really cares about me," I say with hesitation causing me to repeat my words. "He wanted to ruin the audition for me by sitting down here with me. It's over for me. I don't want him in my life anymore…"

I stare at Suzie, realising how similar our backgrounds really are at least similar in our boyfriend situations.

"What's wrong?" Suzie asks.

"I think I'm such an idiot. Here I'm telling you to dump Timothy when I should do similar with Mick," I say. "I think we both need to start over. In whatever way we want to achieve it, whether it's on your own or with someone else, like me with Tommy if he's found and single. Otherwise I think I'm going the same route as you and stay single. It kind of appeals to me to have only myself to care about for a few years…"

"And what if we find Tommy?"

"I'll see how he is," I answer. "If he has changed too much I might pass on rekindling my relationship with him."

Suzie checks her phone for a moment before she comments, "No messages yet from my friend. Sorry…"

"That's okay," I whisper. "I know it may take time. And I know that I may even never find him again. It's really though. I went to the old house where he and I lived, and they demolished it. No one could tell me what happened to the building…"

"Ah that explains my friend's rather cryptic text earlier when she was updating me, when I said that the 'hunt' for Tommy was ongoing," Suzie says. "Unless she says it's okay, I can't tell you her name. It relates to her security clearances or something weird like that…"

"So I guess she's a good person to have on our side when we

become private investigators…" I say, smirking now.

"She's more of a private investigator than either of us might ever be," Suzie comments, laughing loudly.

"Okay, I'm freaking out now about we constantly are talking about everything else than how we can STOP them from being the idiots," I say defiantly. "Maybe we need to determine what we'll DO when we got them up there. And before they come to get us to take part in the audition…"

"Okay, come," Suzie says. "To the back of the green room is the quietest. Let's go over the plan before anyone comes to get you…"

I nod somewhat absentmindedly then I follow Suzie quickly to the corner of the room she'd showed as the best place for us to sit; we'd plan the coming actions later in the day so precisely. A moment later I realise why she chose this spot.

+++

Suzie sits down, and she points at the chair opposite her. I glance around and realise that the chair's placement obscures me from being seen from the door to the green room. If Mick turned up now, I could just stay silent, and it's obvious that Suzie would make an excuse…

She can say I've gone to the restroom or been called for the audition and the idiot would believe her, I think gleefully.

I lean forward to see how much I can see of the door and therefore any potential visitors.

"If someone other than Mick turns up, I'll let you know," Suzie comments. "If it's a guy, I'll ask him what he wants and who he is. You'll be okay. My turn to help you out a bit in return for making me realise I should dump Timothy… Oh, and this is what the loser looks like…"

I stare at the screen of Suzie's cell phone. A dark-haired man the overly white teeth stares back. I feel a chill go down my spine. Something about how he stares at the person who had taken this photo - Suzie perhaps - feels rather unsettling. I glance sideways expecting him to walk in then I quickly lean back in my chair in case it's Mick that might walk in.

"What's wrong?" Suzie asks.

"I feel uncomfortable…" I answer. "It's something about he stares at the camera has me unsettled. When you yelled at Timothy, Mick glanced up over the seats, and said to me that to him he sounds like a stalker…"

"Mick said that?"

"Yeah, and right before we had sex…" I answer.

"So, you really had sex there?" Suzie asked, laughing loudly. "And yeah, maybe Timothy is a stalker in some ways as he spent two months following me like a lost puppy trying to persuade me to date him. Now I think about it all. He was as predatory as they come. And me reading all those damned romance novels convinced me that his behaviour was normal or something stupid like that. I think there need to be some people for once who write a romance that will base it on something better. Like for example, if we find Tommy and he turns out to be a kind and generous guy who treats you like a princess and makes you happy. There should be romance stories like that to be honest…"

Chapter Ten

Glancing at Suzie with a new feeling of hope that things could be better in the future and I suggest, "Why don't you write them?" adding a moment later, "I think you said it yourself. You said the books influenced your perceptions of what true love should be like…"

"Hmm, I might do if the whole thing with finding Tommy has a good outcome," Suzie continues. "If you're okay with it. I won't use your names either. Maybe a great story about true love and such will be a bestseller, and we'll split the income as it's really your story…"

"Or we can write it together?" I suggest.

"Even better, and—"

+++

The door opens, and we both stop speaking immediately. I hold in my breath and lean back as much as I can, and wait while Suzie glances towards the door and I hear a woman speak, "Tash McKinsey…"

I lean forward and answer with, "Yes?"

"They've asked me to come get you. It's your turn. Please leave your bag and coat here."

"I'll look after them," Suzie interjects. "I guess I'm next, right?"

"Yes, that's correct…"

"I see you later, Tash…" Suzie breathes.

Suzie squeezes my hand as she takes hold of both my coat and bag. "And, my dear Tash, break a leg…" she adds a moment later, winking at me playfully.

"Thank you," I whisper, beaming at her. "If things go well, we'll be making plans for our future…"

"I hope so," Suzie says. "Remember which song I told you to sing. I'm certain you'll win the audition with it…"

I walk to the door and before I leave the room I turn, and tell Suzie my decision, "Yes, I'll sing it…"

I feel a knot in my stomach as I approach the left side wings and standing there I hear the muffled sounds of the judges speaking to one another. This is the part of any attempt to be an artist that I absolutely hate. More than before I now wish that Suzie was standing here beside me, and that she could do this performance with me. But if I nailed this performance, I'd be able to decide how and in what format I do future performances—as promised to Suzie and it means she and I can end up team up as Rose Petals…

"McKinsey…"

I breathe deeply when I hear my name called out from the edge of the apron. It's where I'd seen two men line up a row of tables and chairs a few days earlier. The voice that called out is definitely someone with musical training. My ear notes she's a soprano. I step forward and a stage bathed in low lighting greets me. I glance nervously sideways towards where the judges sit. My eyes lock with those of a woman in her mid-forties. Her voice sounds familiar…

"McKinsey?" she questions.

Instinct sets in when in my mind I hear my father's voice, "Be polite and it will open doors for you…"

"Yes ma'am," I answer softly.

"Call me Liz. Please…" she counters.

"Yes… Liz," I say hesitantly.

"Good, good," Liz says. "I understand you're auditioning with a song of your own creation?"

"Yes, I am…" I answer slightly more confidently while my eyes dart over the audience part of the theatre to determine if Mick sits there somewhere looking smug.

"It's called Pretty In Blue…" I answer, perhaps more forcefully than I had intended. I wanted to make certain I had things going my way now. "It's a song—My grandmother wrote the song and gave me the music sheets before she passed away asking me to perform it one day. I was told by Suzie, my friend, to sing it. She's supposed to be my partner in the band I want to—"

"Whenever you're ready…" a male voice from the other end of the table calls out with a bluntness to it I'm unaccustomed to. I take a few minutes to find the mark on the stage where I'm supposed to stand for my performance. I feel deeply nervous now.

"I will sing it a capella as I didn't bring a track with me…" I whisper into the microphone.

This unexpected decision would eliminate Mick totally from the picture. I knew now that if he was somewhere in the audience, he'd be angry. The original plan had been for me to sing a different song, and for him to play a track on his electric piano. This decision to change the plan will make *me* one to decide over whatever will happen next in my life. Fail or win, it's now all on my shoulders…

Fail or win, I must get rid of Mick because I'm determined to determine my destiny…

+++

"McKinsey, go ahead…" I note the encouragement in Liz's voice. "Whenever you're ready…"

I breathe deeply once, close my eyes and start humming in the same way as my grandmother had so often done whenever she'd let me listen to her singing that had been bright, powerful and beautiful to the end. As I sing the words I feel tears well up in my eyes. How I wish she of all people was sitting in the audience listening to me right now. Of all people, I'd known in my life her love had been unconditional, and she'd been the one who had talked to my father to convince him to let me choose my career.

As I sing my confidence grows. My voice swells, and deep fear is replaced by determination.

I want to win this. For me. For Suzie. For me. For grandmother…

Only four minutes later the theatre is silent again, and my heart beat must be audible to all the judges. I stare at them, willing my wish into their mind. I'm almost convinced for a moment that a hand wave from my favourite movie—like Obi-Wan—I could make these judges bend to my will…

"Thank you, McKinsey…"

Momentarily the referencing to me by my last name repeatedly was becoming annoying, but then I remember what my father always told me, "Your family name gives you pride. It's the one thing no one can ever take from you no matter what they try to do…"

I recall the explanation why every first-born of my father's family; myself included and any first child I'd have, would always be registered as a McKinsey. I guess that was another problem I had created between Tommy and myself, I'm realising now. He'd been okay with the idea, especially when he heard where and how the tradition had started. It was me who had been against it, which I realise now that the name gets called out repeatedly.

"Please return to the green room. If we call you up for a second time, it will be to decide our short list," the other woman in the line-up of judges now explains.

She said 'if' not 'when.'

I think bitterly over the words spoken by Liz, and I'm already convincing myself that I'd been unsuccessful just like the previous thirty auditions I'd done in just the last three months. I feel angry in the pit of my stomach, but then Liz's next words have my hopes go overdrive.

"I would like to find you there in an hour to speak to you, okay," Liz says unexpectedly.

I nod profusely and answer, "Yes Liz…"

"You mentioned someone else…" Liz continues. "Have *her* there too…"

I nod again.

"You can go back to the green room."

I'm now annoyed at the man who had spoken earlier. I just didn't like him and had to fight the urge to make this clear to him. But I know that any such behaviour would hamper my success rate in this audition. I feel like he's inserting into a conversation that he has no business to be a part of and that's he's purposely trying to annoying me now…

"Thank you…" I whisper into the microphone. I fumble with the microphone to place it back on the microphone stand, then after a glance each judge imploringly I step back a few steps then spin and rush off the stage with a mind-numbing queasiness rising in my stomach.

I breathe deeply when I reach the left side wings. I grab the curtain beside me, and I squeeze hard. After a few breaths, I feel the queasiness subside. After another minute, it is gone. I never had felt this bad after a performance before. I stumble forward and I don't how long I take to get to the green room but once I'm there; I stare wide-eyed at Suzie.

"Are you okay?"

+++

Suzie helps me the seat I'd been using before going for the audition and lean back staring at the ceiling. I close my eyes for a moment, then I notice Suzie's voice calling out for me from what seems far away.

"Tash… are you okay?"

I breathe deeply again, then I nod, "I think I will be okay. I don't know what happened to me over there. I've never felt this at any audition before today. I think I'm more nervous this time because I know how much I have to rely on this audition. I've just gone against all the plans Mick had for us, then we will fool into leaving me alone later… I just feel so nervous about everything that could go wrong…"

"But you're okay now, right?"

I nod, glancing at the door for a moment. I breathe deeply again, then I decide.

"Mick caused all this by being such a prick with me for all these years," I explain. "Maybe it's time for me to be different now. Maybe we should go with your plan…"

"You mean you had doubts about our plan?" Suzie asks, sounding genuinely surprised now. She leans away from me and stares at me with wide eyes.

"No, not doubts about it just about how well I can pretend to…" I add after a moment. "I was having doubts about myself not you, actually."

"Tash…" Suzie says sharply.

"Yes?"

"Break a leg…"

"Huh what?" I ask.

"Why do people say that, huh?" Suzie asks.

"For luck," I answer. "I guess. I was told in school no one really knows where the saying comes from. The tutor said it was first used over hundred years ago in the roaring twenties. But what has got to do with me and how I feel?"

"But do you know why people would start saying it in the first place?" Suzie asks.

I shake my head.

"I look at you right now. Your face white as a sheet, like you've seen death. All shaking like you're inflicted with illness. All messed up…" Suzie says, holding up a hand to stop me from speaking. "I may have flunked my history exams, but the topic of 'disease' fascinated me in history. I recall from the lessons that during the days of Shakespeare many people would escape from the toils of the day by going to see theatre performances. My personal theory is that people thought you could get the plague from breaking a leg. So people said 'break a leg' to people who they saw as rivals. And then hoped that they'd break a leg, get ill with the plague and die…"

"Ewww, gross," I comment.

"I doubt that it's true but at some point something happened to make certain that turned the expression lucky instead of an expression of bad luck," Suzie continues. "You didn't bat an eyelid when I said. Ten centuries ago I'd be a rival, but now we're working on working together and setting our own destiny into action…"

"I guess you're right," I say, and I grin at Suzie.

Oddly Suzie had set my mind at ease with a silly story that I know to be fiction. As I listen to her explanations, I sit up more and feel the tension leave my body and suddenly the whole idea of deceiving Mick and Timothy in a switcheroo didn't sound so bad anymore.

"So, I guess we're really doing it?" I ask.

"If you're referring to our plan, if you want it to happen then yes, we'll do it…" Suzie answers. "To be honest, I was scared about doing all of it as much as you seem to be…."

I stare at Suzie for a moment, then I smile and say, "Suzie…"

"Yes?"

"Break a leg…" I say.

"Why are you saying that now?"

I nudge my head sideways. Suzie follows my gaze then blurts out, "Oh, right…"

The woman from before stands at the door and now shows her impatience by tapping her watch a few times and Suzie jerks to her feet.

In her effort to settle my mind, Suzie ignored the fact that her turn, as the last candidate in the auditions, is coming now…

Chapter Eleven

Suzie stares at the woman at the door, then she whispers towards me, "I feel so yucky all the sudden…"

Suzie exhales, then continues, "I know the feeling. It's the nerves. I feel yucky…" she whispers. "I never thought I'd feel this way ever going in front of an audience…"

"I know the feeling," I whisper to Suzie, copying a few of her words. "But I think I nailed it by singing Pretty In Blue as my audition song. Pay very close attention to woman Liz and ignore the rest of them and you'll be fine…"

"What's so special about Liz, whoever she is…?" Suzie asks.

"Listen to her voice when she speaks. Remember the song playing while we were eating this morning in the cafeteria," I continue. "It will all make sense… And Suzie, break a leg…"

It's Suzie's turn to find courage deep inside her. This moment of finding courage is a good way for both of us to find the courage we will need later when we're ready to execute our plans later…

+++

Suzie leaves the room, and now it's my turn to contemplate like she might have been doing while she'd waited for *me* to return with the news of outcome of my audition. I'm certain she'll be okay in her audition, but until we were free of the two annoyingly interfering boyfriends, nothing was certain about the future afterwards. I hope more than before that things will be okay. I pull the contract from my bag, and I stare intently at the first page for several minutes and remember the words said by Liz.

"She wants to see my contract…" I mumble. "But why…?"

I study the contract thoroughly. Nothing stands out that would make me weary of its content. I'm rather puzzled why Liz is so interested in its content. I glance up when realisation hits me about why she sounded so familiar, "That was her on the radio at the cafeteria earlier. She's a famous singer. No wonder she doesn't tell her last name. Might she be Liz James?"

I shrug my shoulders a moment, then I almost jump when the door opens and Liz steps into the green room.

"Hello Tash, I don't have long but I wanted to read the contract to determine if you need to find a lawyer, or more precisely a different lawyer," Liz says as an explanation for visiting me in the green room between the auditions and something actually not permitted by the rules of the event. "Regardless of the outcome of today's events, you need to be prepared for the possibilities of how life could go for you. You will need two separate contracts. One that will cover your rights and that protects your grandmother's legacy, and another contract to cover both of you if you're sure about forming a band with your friend Suzie… She will soon perform so I have a few minutes to check over your contract. Is this it?"

I hand the sheets of paper to Liz without saying a word for several minutes, then I pluck up the courage to ask her…

"Are you Liz James?"

"Hush… No one is supposed to know that until performance night…" Liz says, grinning before sitting down. "There are times an artist such as myself would want to stay anonymous. I go by my birth name in my home city. Only a few there would recognise me without all this makeup plastered on my face."

Liz points to her face, then studies me, "You don't wear makeup?" she asks.

"You're the second person to ask me," I answer. "Mick won't let me wear it…"

"Oh, was he the person you would perform with originally?" Liz asks. "That's why we were quizzing you before you started.

According to our notes, it listed Tash McKinsey and Mick Sutterfield were performing a duet... Were your plans changed for any reason...?"

"I changed my mind about doing stuff with him..." I admit. "I think I wanted something better... Something different."

"Did Suzie change your mind?"

"Yes and no..."

"Did she influence your decisions?" Liz asks with some urgency in her voice.

"In a way she did but not for the reasons you may think," I answer forcefully. "I've been wanting to be in control of my destiny for a while. I went on my own to get this contract sorted..."

"Somehow you've been fooled into believing you control your career..." Liz says. "Are you sure your lawyer doesn't know your boyfriend?"

I frown and stare hard at the papers in Liz's hands. Suddenly I wasn't so sure.

"Why are you here?" I blurt out. "I'm going to get disqualified if they find out you spoke to me..."

Liz ignores my protests and explains why she's asking.

"Whenever you take part in an audition with US, you're vetted beforehand. It's so we can determine whether you're an artist with an existing career, or not," Liz says. "In your case, the vetting process uncovered this contract. It requires a lawyer to file a public copy of the contract with one organisation representing artists. When you applied to this audition, they sent us the contract. I read it and although I'm no expert on law matters, I know when a contract is valid or not. You need a better lawyer, Tash. Find a lawyer you can trust thoroughly..."

I sense the urgency in Liz's words. Like the topic might affect her.

"Did your career get screwed over by the wrong contract?" I ask hesitantly.

Liz nods once then says, "I don't that for someone so talented as you. Did your grandmother ever write a score for the song you performed?"

I shake my head. I based my singing of the song on

remembering her singing it once when I was maybe five or six years old, and I've never been certain I was singing it correctly whenever I sang it in later years. The last time my grandmother had sung it must have been almost twenty years ago, only a few weeks before she died so unexpectedly.

"To sing a song this complex a cappella and from memory is hard for the most skilled singers," Liz continues. "But doing it without the training to be an 'a cappella' singer is remarkable. Singing in that way requires a certain skill…"

"I knew I botched it up halfway…" I admit.

"Despite it, you sang it so well that I wanted to talk with you about your career options…" Liz says. "It states here you have secured a band name—Rose Petals. Have you got the paperwork for it with you?"

I nod and reach in the bag and pull a dark brown unopened envelope from it.

"Ah, it's sealed. Keep it that way until you've secured a better contract…" Liz says while her hand stops me from opening the envelope.

"Why is that?" I ask.

"This is an official document that secures your recording name. If there is anything is this contract that was put in to allow Mick Sutterfield access to the name, whether it is earnings from royalties, control over the material you write, or who you sing with it can make things hard for you later on," Liz explains. "Are you going to keep him around or are you working on a way to get him out of your life? I think I met him on my way here. He doesn't sound like a good influence to be honest…"

"Actually… Suzie is helping me to get rid of him," I admit. "She's got a same problem with her boyfriend. At least, I think it's the case…"

"I'll keep it in mind when I listen to her performance…" Liz says reassuringly. "How *did* the two of you meet?"

When I hear a snort from Liz, it's obvious I must blush bright red. I decide not to tell Liz how Suzie and I had indulged in some lesbian fantasy in the rest room four floors below us. Somehow I don't think she'd understand the reasons and for both of us, it was mostly a release of frustration that had led us to behaving in that way…

"She heard me practising my song. The one I sang for the audition," I say, and I hope it's believed. "She suggested I sing it rather than what I had planned."

"And your first choice wasn't your choice, I guess?" Liz asks.

"My boyfriend pressured me to sing other stuff..." I answer, looking down. "I don't think he'll be happy with what I did..."

"That is why I suggested you secure your recording name, and also your rights..." Liz continues. "Otherwise there will be those who'll take advantage of you. Find a lawyer you can trust, and soon. And to answer your question about my career... Yes, someone screwed up my career, but it never stopped me in my efforts to build a career. Long haul is the way to go about it, rather than going for quick fame like your boyfriend seems to think is the route."

"I guess I got something in mind that will solve that problem," I say, smiling conspiratorially at Liz. "It's maybe better, I don't tell you how I will fix things for myself. But Suzie will help with it. I will not let the idiot screw up any future I got possible for myself..."

"Yes, I think it's best I'm left in the dark..." Liz says before she glances at her watch and then gets up. "I guess I have to go before I'm missed. It's actually against the rules for the judges to talk with those competing for a placement but I found your case compelling enough for me to come speak with you. Be weary of who you deal with from here on. Never make the mistakes I made, or that your grandmother made..."

She knows about my grandmother? How...? I frown for a moment, but then I remember that I had mentioned it in my introduction for Pretty In Blue. I told them it was my grandmother's song. I realise now that Liz was warning me so I didn't loose any control over it. *Maybe make certain that the song stays in my control even if I go in business with Suzie. I only met her today. I don't know how much I can trust her. Not yet at least. Not until I know for certain she knows how to find Timothy...*

"Liz, can I ask how you got screwed over?" I say hesitantly.

Liz nods.

"How?" I ask again.

"I was once young like you. And perhaps too naïve for my good. I relied too much on a man who promised me he'd marry me one day," Liz says coldly, and it's obvious from her voice she's still bitter about what had happened to her. "If that was your boyfriend sitting near us and who called out to us, he's trouble. He tried to force us to choose you and made it absolutely clear your choice displeased him to sing Pretty In Blue. IF you can rid yourself of him, you're better off. I'm not interested in finding out how you two met, but his behaviour reminds me of how George—that was who I would marry—behaved to me and which led to me walking away from a wedding that was just days away. I've never regretted doing it. Suzie sounds like she's utterly loyal towards you. I don't know how the two of you met, but you might have a friend for life there that you'll be able to trust. If I had had someone like her, I might never even gotten engaged to George. Luckily the person who said he's your boyfriend had walked away when she arrived because I don't think he'd appreciate what she said…"

"What did she say?" I whisper.

"She told me not to tell you but I will say it anyway," Liz continues. "Apparently, she's got a friend and just before you got back here she got a text saying she's *found* Tommy—Whoever he is I hope he's a better choice than whoever shouted at me and the other judges."

"He's someone I shouldn't have left…" I whisper.

"If that's the case then I suggest you go find him," Liz says. "Don't make the wrong choices. Rid yourself of the so-called boyfriend trying to dictate how you should live your life and find the better person."

"I will… Thank you," I whisper, smiling at Liz.

"I have to go now," Liz says. "I guess that because we're still inside the theatre for me to say 'Break a leg' is a better choice to tell you… well, you know…"

I nod and grin broadly before saying, "I will make certain it is on my side in all the choices I make from now on. Thank you so much for your advice…"

Chapter Twelve

I watch Liz walk from the room and stare for several minutes at the closed door. Suddenly, everything felt different. Suddenly, it made sense to help in the 'plan' suggested by Suzie.

It makes sense for us to deceive them both. It might be fun, too. Not sure how the future will look afterwards, but I guess I must deal with it when I'm rid of Mick…

It would solve everything that stood between my plan to have a career as a singer and what I was dealing with right now. I smile maliciously. Suddenly, Suzie's plan was fun. All the previous worries about this plan disappeared from my mind.

I straighten up and look towards the door and wonder when Suzie may be back. I hear footsteps and I hold my breath to discover who might enter the green room now. It's Suzie…

I breathe out, relieved as, for a moment, I'd feared Mick would come barging in. After what Liz had said about him, I know now how he had reacted to my assertive behaviour at the audition which had screwed up his ideas of what we should do in terms of my career…

This is my career really and why the hell is Mick even dictating how it goes like Liz pointed out?, I think and I feel overwhelming anger deep inside me because I finally realise how right Liz and Suzie are in each of their assessment of my situation. *Not for him to decide how my career should go. Tommy was never like this ever. The last time he and I talked, he told me to decide for myself what I wanted to do and that he'd support all my decisions. Yet I walked away from him. I guess I was afraid of fully committing to him…*

+++

Suzie opens the door, and she smiles at me with obvious delight. I immediately attempt to hide my dismay about what Liz had told me half an hour ago. Suzie's presence takes away some worry I'm feeling, but not all of it disappears. I smile back at Suzie who seems oblivious of any worry I'm feeling…

"Right, I stayed behind for a bit and tried to hear what they were saying. Apparently, the plan is for five of all candidates to be selected, and there are two hundred candidates they're selecting from," Suzie explains in hushed tones. "I really hope you're one of them. Liz said that even if we don't win, we have all the tools in our hands to make our own career. Whatever she means with that comment. Her comment caused the other judges to stare at her with annoyance. I had a hard time not to laugh at what I saw happening between them…"

"I think I know what she's referring to," I hiss at Suzie. "I think your plan for us to rid us of the two annoying boyfriends has to work because then we can go forward with the rest of our lives and start making a singing career together."

"I guess it can also involve some FUN for us…" Suzie says conspiratorially, and she beams at me before she adds, "I think WE deserve such fun…"

"I… errr… I want to do it," I stutter. The momentary certainty from minutes ago has all but evaporated from me for a moment. "Liz said that having Mick around will not help me. I'll explain later what's going on…"

"Fair enough," Suzie says while deciding to make my long hair the object of her attention and curling her finger around a strand hanging in front of my face. "We will rid you of the pesky boyfriend before the day is over. I can assure you of that happening today… No matter what I want you to be sorted out… Liz mentioned in her spat at the other judges about your song being unique enough for you to get a good career out of all this, and I'm determined now to want to help you so you can make it happen sooner rather than later. First, we rid you of the pesky boyfriend. Second, we find the one true love you're searching for..."

"Tommy is probably married with kids by now..." I grunt, looking annoyed towards Suzie who frowns now.

"Or he is single, and he's looking for you," Suzie quips, ignoring the displeasure in my voice. WE need a plan..."

"I thought we already had one..."

"Not to rid you off your loser boyfriend, for what you wear for your big day..." Suzie says, beaming.

"Huh, what?"

"You want to marry Tommy when we find him, right?" Suzie asks, adding a moment later, "You're damned right I want this to end with a happy ever after. You deserve that more than even I do..."

"You deserve it as much..." I protest.

"I guess so... But fixing it all for you is easier," Suzie mumbles, looking down now. She places her hand on my knee and for a few moments I wish it to go closer to my pussy. For her to do what she'd done earlier in the day. Because it would distract me from the thoughts of doom going through my mind. It's obvious now she feels an attraction towards me that she's keeping under control. I'm guessing that's the reason her hand caresses my leg for a few moments before she jerks and pulls her hand away...

I take Suzie's hand and study her face for several minutes, then I ask what had been on my mind for at least the last three hours, "What do you want to have for yourself from all of this? Please, let me tell what's going on that made you talk to me in the first place?"

"I want to live my life with no commitments other than my work as a singer," Suzie answers. "I cannot explain it better than that. I'm just fed up of the obligations of being in a relationship. Single life is my goal... Your goal SHOULD be a career as a musician, and to be with Tommy if that's something you also want. From what you've told me about him, he sounds like a decent guy..."

Suzie makes me smile, and she lightens my mood with the comment, and it encourages me to share my thoughts of doom with her now.

"Okay, where can we go to get this plan into action?" I ask next. I glance towards the door and add hastily, "I think Liz knows something is up with us, but she said she didn't want to get involved. She did warn me to be careful with how Mick is behaving…"

"Wow, I'm amazed she would do that…" Suzie hisses. "And that she noticed it about him. We HAVE to sort things out so we can leave without either of them and create our own futures, or as it's the case with you… set you back on track in a future with the guy you're supposed to be with…"

I smirk at Suzie when I realise what she's suggesting and I blurt out, "So how will I explain to Tommy if I've just helped you with seducing Timothy. I might blurt out the wrong name during love making…"

"Are you comfortable getting naked in front of strangers?" Suzie asks. "Like you might have to do for costume changes during a concert…"

"Yeah, I understand what you're saying…" I whisper.

"Well, consider this a practice run… Actually, it will be a practice run for both of us," Suzie adds after a pause in which she contemplates our options. I never thought I'd get today in my life when the word 'our' would revolve around something other than my life with Timothy…"

"Or me with Mick," I mumble.

"So you want him gone then?" she asks me with a conspiratorial edge to her voice.

"If you got any plans to make happen, I don't want to know about it," I grunt. "I rather be in the dark about whatever you do to make it happen. It would—It's more fun that way. Neither of us can then be accused of planning any of this."

I smirk when Suzie glances towards me with curiosity written over her face. I will not tell her that one of my kinks is to sleep with a best friend's lover…

+++

Leaning back staring up at the stomach-curdling green ceiling of the 'green room' and yes, the thought enters my mind why someone took the words so literally, I contemplate my kink. I suggested to Suzie that it would be better that we didn't tell one another what each has planned precisely to deal the other person's boyfriend. I realise now also that I figured out a small part of why I had just packed up and moved out from Tommy…

And so Suzie had left me alone finally after we went over the broad strokes of 'the plan' one more time. And then I was alone with my thoughts, *Dammit, Suzie, I keep confusing between your loser boyfriend Timothy and my Tommy because their names are so similar,* I think as I frown at the thought. *It's almost like some stupid thing from one of your books with two characters with a similar name. I guess I understand why authors don't do similar names for their characters. That was the worst romance novel I had to read over the last few days, but I guess I'm getting too polite to Suzie as she's finding Tommy...*

The whole damned situation seems a cliche now when I think about it. *Who the hell goes around doing a revenge scam on their boyfriend anyway...?*

I glance at the door when someone knocks on the door. I get up and twist my chair ninety degrees so I'm not noticed by whoever sticks their head into the room. I hold my breath.

Another knock.

They open the door.

I stay silent when a familiar voice calls out, "Tash... are you in here?"

I don't want Mick to find me here right now. Now I feel like I don't even want to see him any more. He's a loser and all his actions, as described by Liz earlier, had proved it to me how badly he would affect my career options or my chance at making something of my band Rose Petals if he's involved or has any say in it.

I quickly glance around me to determine there's nothing around the room that might show him I was here before or that I'm here now. I feel relief when I see my bag and coat to my right - out of his view.

I sit rigidly on the chair and hope it doesn't squeak at any point until he's gone.

"Tash..."

Dammit, go away already, I think, now frowning with deep annoyance at the presence of a man who'd controlled most of my decisions for the last several years. If Suzie's stupid romance novels taught me anything, it's that I need to make my own decisions and not have some control freak wreck my life for me. *Tommy was like that with me…*

A few footsteps go towards the door, then the door closes and the footsteps fade away. I glance hastily around the corner and see the room empty. But only a moment later I jump almost out of my chair when the door swings open and both Liz and Suzie walk in deep in conversation. They go silent and stare at me, confused.

"You look like you saw a ghost…" Liz quips, trying to hide her bemusement at my reaction.

"I think I did…" I hiss. "Did he see you? Either of you?"

"Who?" Suzie asks.

"Mick…" I answer. "He was here just now. He called out for me. I don't think he saw me…"

"He's in a restricted part of the theatre if he was snooping around here," Liz says, now sounding almost like a teacher reprimanding a school kid. I suppress a giggle. Liz's expression is deadly serious and remember our earlier conversation as our eyes locks.

"Can you keep him away from here, Liz?" Suzie asks. "I don't he's good news. He'll interfere with Tash's plans for Rose Petals."

"Ah, so you're going ahead with the plans…" Liz says, smiling. "With Suzie or on your own?"

"We're teaming up," I answer. "Suzie is fast becoming a good friend. Without her suggestions I wouldn't have weighed up my options and realised I can do much better than having Mick in my life…"

"She will be the boss," Suzie blurts out, beaming at each of us. "Tash has way more talent than I ever will have and she deserves to become famous and all that…"

"Don't underestimate your own skills, Suzie," Liz says as she places a hand on Suzie's shoulder motherly.

"Have you seen her notebooks, Liz?" Suzie protests. "Tash has enough songs written for the next twenty albums at least. She's the one with the talent, and I want her to succeed. If I enjoy it, it's only because I believed in her from the start…"

Chapter Thirteen

Suzie and I hastily follow Liz through the empty theatre as she speeds towards 'her office upstairs' where she's going to teach us some of the lessons she'd learned from being in the music business for the last few decades. Suzie and I glance for a moment when we approach a lift and in what almost seems to feel like a scene from some sort of spy movie Liz taps in a number code on a key pad to the left of the lift.

"Hurry before anyone sees us," Liz hisses conspiratorially.

Suzie and I dive into the lift, and just as she will also enter the lift we hear a voice call out.

"Hey lady, have you seen my girlfriend by chance?"

"SHIT," I hiss before a hand quickly covers my mouth tightly and stops the rest of my shouts. It's Suzie's hand that keeps me silent as Liz walks away from the lift. We listen to her talking to Mick and as the conversation continues on my panic sets in and I almost expect for him to barge past Liz and be standing at the lift doors with glaring eyes and seething anger towards me.

I panic even more when the lift doors suddenly close and the conversation between Liz and Mick becomes a series of muffled sounds that don't tell me anything about what he wants or why he wanted to speak to Liz.

A hand taps my shoulder, and when I glance at Suzie, she has her finger covering over her lips while still covering my mouth. I nod at her once. She removes her hand and walks to the doors and leans in, obviously to listen to whatever is being said. I stand frozen in place. If Mick hears Suzie walking, he'll assume one person is in the lift and not two. If he asks, Liz might get away with suggesting it's just Suzie waiting in the lift.

"Try the buttons…" I hiss.

"Shh," Suzie hisses.

"Try—the—buttons…" I hiss under my breath. "We—can—make—him—think—the—lift—was—called."

As I try to tell Suzie my idea, I'm pausing between each word to make sure I'm not heard outside. Suzie stares at me for a moment, then she comprehends what I'm going on about and she presses the top button on the panel to her left.

Nothing happens.

She grunts audibly, then presses the next button. Or should I say she slams it?

We both jump when the lift springs into action with a bell sound. It moves for the next thirty seconds, then it stops and the doors open onto a spacious room. Suzie and I glance at one another and she asks, "Where are we?"

"Maybe this is Liz's office…" I suggest, chuckling softly. "Or we're somewhere that we shouldn't be," I add a moment after.

"I'm certain Liz will find us," Suzie says, then she steps into the 'office' that looks more like a film set for some posh drama movie than an office. After a pause, I copy Suzie's actions. We turn when a moment later the lift doors slam shut.

"SHIT!"

I laugh out loudly at Suzie's sudden annoyance and I say, "It was your idea…"

"Yeah but what if the lift comes back and Liz and Mick stand inside it," Suzie quips. My stare at her tells her how annoyed I am with her suggestion of events.

"Nooo…" I gasp

"Naah, I don't think Liz is the type to trample over someone's trust," Suzie reassures me. "I think that's why she's protective of you, of us… She's likely been through something similar that she sees happening between you and loser boyfriend Mick…"

"I hope she's okay," I whisper, staring at the closed doors of the lift.

"I don't think she will let Mick into the lift," Suzie says. "Did you see the top button? It's present on this pad too… Look over there…"

I glance at the keypad beside lift doors and see an oddly shaped larger button, "What's that for?" I ask.

"I'm guessing… something like a panic button," Suzie suggests. "Okay, I'm really guessing now, but if this is like a regular security system, like for example in a shop, I would guess Liz just needs to hit it once and someone comes to her downstairs. They'll sort out Mick and STOP him from coming up here…"

"Hmm, I guess so," I grunt before I glance once more around the spacious room. Then I spot something that causes my eyes to light up and for me to feel happier.

"A guitar…" I blurt out.

"Huh, what?" Suzie asks.

"A guitar," I repeat, pointing at the soft in the room's corner. Suzie looks towards where I'm pointing. "Can you play one?" she asks.

I nod, then rush to the sofa and sit down beside the instrument. I gently touch the glossy dark wood it's made of and my finger twangs a note. I smile at Suzie who pauses then sits down on the edge of the solid wooden coffee table near me.

"Play something…" Suzie whispers.

I nod and gingerly lift the instrument from the sofa and place it in front of me. My fingers do a few tests for finger memory to determine if I could still play the guitar. Then an idea comes to my mind. Earlier, during the auditions, I had sung Pretty In Blue a capella to the judges… mostly to show them I had skill as a singer, even with no music present. Now I could also show my musical prowess.

The combination of singing the song with the musical score that I had written for it over the last three months of living with Tommy influences Suzie. After I sing the first verse, she has tears flowing down her cheeks and a mellow smile around her lips. Once she's heard the chorus once she joins in when I sing it for a second time. After the third verse she's singing the chorus in her own unique way that adds a new dimension to the song that takes me aback somewhat.

Once the song has ended Suzie and I stare with shared emotions at one another, grinning. This is the FUN we'd been looking for ever since meeting one another... not the nonsense involving either of our respective loser boyfriends...

My hand moves over the strings and a moment later we're singing Pretty In Blue once more. But now we're doing it together, and to accompany my guitar play Suzie stamps her foot and taps her fingers on the table. Slowly I believe we could pull it off if ever she and I were to perform this song to a proper audience...

We're silent when the song ends for the fourth time, then both of us jump up when Liz speaks, "That was amazing to hear it with guitar play to go with it..."

"How long have you been here?" I blurt out.

"Long enough for me to hear two talented people who need the best people helping them to make a name for themselves," Liz answers. "First, we sort out that contract of yours. I'm not a legal expert but I've read enough of them over the years to know what should and shouldn't be in one..."

"Is this your guitar?" I ask shyly. "I hope you don't mind it I borrowed it..."

"Of course not," Liz says. "It was a gift from my father when I got my first gig sorted out. I was maybe a year or two younger than you are now... Use the guitar for as long as we're here still and whenever you want to check the music you've written for your songs, okay?"

I nod, but hastily place the guitar back on the sofa when Liz walks to the desk nearby and sits down behind it. Suzie and I dive for each of the chairs in front of the desk. I grab my bag from the desk where I'd placed it somewhat absentmindedly on arriving and pull from it the contract I'd secured only days before finding out about the rehearsals at this concert hall. I hand it to Liz who nods and leans back and spends the next ten minutes silently reading the content on the six sheets of paper...

My anxiety heightens every time I see a frown on her face, then she looks up and stares at me for several minutes.

"Who wrote this?" Liz asks.

"I did and then I told the lawyer that's what I wanted as a contract," I answer nervously.

"You had no legal training?" Liz asks.

"Well, not me. Tommy did, and he'd bore me endlessly with stuff about his studies," I answer and I glance sideways when I notice Suzie tap her cell phone for something, but my attention shifts back to Liz when she asks her next question. "But you didn't study law, right?" she asks.

I shake my head, feeling confused now.

"I think this is the best damned legal document I've seen written up by someone with no legal knowledge in the last two decades," Liz says. I notice pride in her voice, like she's my mother praising me for good exam results or something like it. "But even so, you need someone with proper legal knowledge look it over. Do you have contact with this… Tommy? Who is he anyway?"

"It was her boyfriend…" Suzie grunts teasingly. I shoot an annoyed stare at her to be met by a wink.

"Yes, it was my boyfriend," I answer. "Not had any contact with him in years."

"You'll see him again," Suzie breathes as she glances down at her cell phone. I eye her cell phone from the corner of my eye to see if I can see if it has any messages displayed from her mysterious Polish private investigator. She sees me…

"No, Tash, no messages about him in case you wondered. Why didn't you tell me he was studying for a law degree?" Suzie says accusingly. "It's such a small detail to make it easier to find someone…"

"Are you looking for Tommy?" Liz enquires.

"Not you too…" I blurt out, rolling my eyes. "Yes, I happen to be looking for him. It's her fault I'm doing. She suggested he'd be better for me as a boyfriend rather than Mick."

"And… is he?" Liz continues.

I look from person to person, defeated by the logic of the situation. I stare aimlessly at the window for several minutes, contemplating the situation. Did I really want to find him or is what I'm doing just dreaming? Would I enjoy having him around still…?

"I think he could help me fix my contract or know someone who could…" I mumble. "If I can find him…" I glance at Suzie with pleading eyes then I add, "… If SHE can find him… Your friend that is… Please, find him for me…"

Suzie's puzzled face melts to compassion, and she nods, "She's calling every person she knows for information that may help her find him. Knowing he had been studying to become a lawyer will make it easier because he needs to be registered to practise law in whatever country he lives in. She'll call me when she has found him. When that happens I'll tell you immediately…"

"I guess I was right earlier when I said that you two are showing true friendship towards one another," Liz comments. "You could almost be sisters if I didn't know any better."

"I'm an only child," Suzie says.

"I have only… one sister who writes books, and she—," I add to Suzie's answer. "Well, she's who encouraged me to pursue a career as a singer when she caught me singing in the shower…"

Suzie laughs loudly when she hears my explanation for how I began singing.

"Is that the only reason?" Liz asks, sounding more serious.

"No," I continue. "I was in school and when we had to choose subjects, I was rude to the teacher about leaving out music lessons and singing as choices on the form. I got detention, but when my father had talked down the principle about what had happened, they added the topics. They made me check everyone's musical skill and when we had thirty people for the classes, that's when I learned to sing and play music properly…"

"Hence why you could play that guitar so well," Suzie comments.

I nod to confirm Suzie is right in her assessment, then continue my explanation. It's the first time since before I met Tommy I've felt comfortable to open up to others about my life choices. I will guess already that the rest of my story - the parts I had kept from Suzie in our earlier conversations - will cause her to feel either shock or disbelief towards me.

Not everyone gets a sob story like mine and then gets a second chance at life afterwards offered to them with a friendly hand being offered towards them by a total stranger who was a good person really, I think bitterly thinking back now at the real reason I'd even met Tommy in the first place…

Chapter Fourteen

I glance down for several minutes because I'm unsure how to start telling my story in the first place. Each time I think I can start talking about the day when I happened to have landed in Tommy's lap - in the literal sense as I now recall - I clam up and stop myself from speaking.

A hand covers over my hand gently. I look up and it seems Suzie has turned her chair ninety degrees towards me and she's staring at me with such compassion I feel my eyes sting with the beginnings of tears. I glance in the other direction when another hand, somewhat colder and rougher, touches me from the other side. I stare at Liz's eyes that speak volumes of knowing my current emotions. I'm certain now I'm not the first girl she'd had to deal with in this way in the two decades of her career as a musician.

"I guess—" I say but I stop speaking before something deep inside me finds courage I never realised that I had in the first place as I say to Liz, "I guess you know what my story is like…"
She nods curtly.
"I don't think I'd be here if Tommy hadn't found me that day…" I whisper.
"You didn't say any of this earlier…" Suzie says, but she doesn't sound angry and when I glance at her, it shows she feels something different about what I'm trying to tell. "Did something bad happen to you, Tash?"
I nod once.
"Tell us," Liz urges. "It will help if you tell about it instead of

keeping it bottled up.”

I glance at Suzie before I say toward her, “Remember how I said I felt uncomfortable about our plan?”

“What plan?” Liz snaps. “Oh never mind, don’t tell me. If it’s some scheme to get rid of your boyfriends, I don’t even want to know about it. I can guess well enough what the plan could be, but the less I know…”

Liz’s voice trails off in a series of mumbles and angry grunts and neither Suzie nor I react to it just in case she’s angry with us and before I can say anything more Liz adds, “IF you will do something make sure you won’t regret the end result. Make sure you don’t lose your dignity over it. BE careful, okay. And do nothing that will hamper your chances at a career… OKAY? This goes for both of you… OKAY?”

Suzie and I glance at one another, then we seem to nod at the same time.

“Let me tell both of you my story first,” Liz blurts out. “Before you tell yours…” Liz squeezes my hand gently. “I was once your age and full of hopes and dreams. They almost took it from me when an irate fan barged into the changing room during a concert. The man who became my husband saved my life he’s still deeply protective every day. You met him. He was sitting somewhat behind me during the judging. The one who was wearing a purple hat…”

“I remember him,” Suzie quips. “Sorry if I giggled when it was my turn to perform. I found the hat amusing…”

“There’s a reason he wears this specific hat of all hats,” Liz continues. “He wore it on the day he stopped the fan, and he says it’s my good luck charm. If it wasn’t for him, the fan would have smashed that up…” Liz points to the guitar, adding, “You know already how special the guitar is for me. He and I started dating a week after the concert ended. Three months later he and I married.”

“Are you still married?” I ask, glancing at Liz’s hand resting over my hand. I spot a white gold ring on it.

“Yes, and it’s a happy marriage,” Liz says. “No kids as neither of us wanted any but I’ve vowed that instead I help girls and women in this industry succeed and be safe.”

“Sounds like a good thing to do with all the ‘me too’ shit that’s been in the news in the last several years,” Suzie says then she squeezes my hand tighter and whispers, "… Sorry for what I did on the first day when we met…"

"It's okay," I quip. "I didn't mind it actually…"

I grin broadly at Suzie then beam at Liz too who seems confused for a moment before saying, "Okay, another thing I don't want to be told about, okay…"

"Suzie and I just had a bit of fun," I blurt out.

"We were talking about you meeting Tommy," Liz interjects.

My smile disappears immediately, but Liz's comment makes me feel somewhat better deep inside as it hints at a similar situation as the one I had been in.

"I don't want to go into too many of the details but what Suzie said about 'me too' is, kind of, what happened to me," I whisper. "It left me in a bad situation and terrified. Tommy found me and took me to the hospital. I was okay… errr…"

I glance down, then look up at Liz again. She nods knowingly. I'm now certain she understands what I'm hinting at with my glance and the feelings of hesitation being clear in me telling my story.

"Once I was okay, he took me home with him," I continue. "He lived at home with his parents still. His mother gave me the room with a lock on the door so I could shut it and keep the world outside and feel safe. He, and also his mother, slowly helped me get in a better place even if it was hard for them dealing with a girl who'd been overdosed in a date rape…"

"That's terrible…" Suzie whispers. "Are you certain about our plan still?"

"Yes I am," I answer. "I think it will help me get over that part of my past… And no, I won't go into the details of our plans, Liz, as promised…"

"Well, from everything you said I will guess you plan to have sex with your boyfriend and then dump him," Liz says.

I don't respond so not to let Liz know she's wrong with her assessment.

"Make sure you don't get pregnant," Liz adds a moment later. "I've seen enough girls end up that way and then regret the consequences because they had to choose their career or a baby…"

"I have contraception. I live on the road actually mostly, and the guys in bands where I ended up as a backup singer aren't too polite about it when you say 'no' to them after a night of booze," I whisper.

"I know it's not that way all the time, but it takes just a few nasty ones to end up always looking over your shoulders for the next time it could happen…"

"Hence why Jake always sits behind me wearing his purple hat," Liz whispers.

"Jake is your husband, right…?" Suzie asks.

"He is…"

+++

After pouring out every emotion I had festering inside me, Liz gets up and pulls me to my feet. She leads me to the sofa where she pushes me down beside the guitar.

"I think it's time for YOU to have fun instead of dwelling on the gloom and doom of life," Liz quips, beaming at Suzie and myself. "What other talent have you been hiding from us…"

Liz winks at Suzie, and it causes me to feel the need to grin teasingly at Suzie about it. She retaliates by telling Liz about my notebooks, "… There are hundreds of poems and lyrics in her notebooks, Liz," Suzie comments, grinning. "She has *true* talent the world should know about…"

"Really? Show me your notebooks…" Liz says.

I get up and grab hold of my bag realising now that my whole life of the last several years was contained in my bag, and that I'd guarded its content from being seen - ever - by Mick, who'd often enough been curious about its content. *Every time he asked, I refused. But why was that? Was I afraid of what he'd discover about my life? I never told him about Tommy…*

I sit down opposite of Suzie and Liz, and after a pause I open my bag and pull out my bundle of notebooks. I caress over the cover of the top notebook. Which shows the beautiful drawing of a bundle of roses I drew over the last six weeks.

"Artistic too, I see…" Liz says, beaming a smile at me.
"If possible, I'd want this on the cover of one album," I whisper.

"If that's possible at all…"

"I can try to arrange it if you're selected…" Liz says. "I still have to say 'if' because I've not had a discussion with the other judges yet. But don't worry… you have *my* back… Even if it's a 'no' I will help both of you succeed, okay…"

I smile weakly, but I know Liz is right and I nod.

I hand the notebooks Liz who runs her hand over the cover then she opens to the first page listing the words of Pretty In Blue. Liz's eyes move over the page several times, then she glances up at me. She turns the page and looks the next two pages for even longer, then she nods and turns the page once more.

Every page turns makes me more anxious but also curious about what her thoughts are… Unlike reading a book where I can see the thoughts of another person in the book as a reader, I cannot know Liz's thoughts. It kind of annoys me for a moment, but then I decide it's probably better. Like before, when I never knew the real thoughts of all those guys at any gig…

"How many songs are there?" Liz asks, and I startle somewhat at the urgency in her voice.

"I think I've written songs since I started singing lessons at school," I explain. "I think… It's something like two or three hundred. Not all of them are completed though. Maybe a third of them are complete songs…"

"Are you planning to complete more of them?" Liz asks.

I nod and continue, "If I have enough time to do that…"

"If you get selected you'll spend six months preparing for your first concert. Both of you based on what you had planned with Rose Petals. Besides your first concert, you'll also record between twelve and fifteen songs for your first album," Liz says. "I will help you, this will still be the same thing though the first time you'll perform is as a guest artist. They book my next concert for January next year…"

"That will give us just over ten months to learn all the songs," Suzie says. "Well, for me to learn them because probably already know them very well…"

"I'll help you with it," I say proudly, smiling at Suzie delightfully. "You picked up the rhythm and words for Pretty In Blue faster than

I thought it would be possible…"

"Though I had to listen a few times before I picked up the rhythm of the song," Suzie admits. "The song is way more complex than you might realise, especially in the music for it…"

Liz grabs the guitar and holds it out to me, saying, "Play the music for a few more of the songs listed here," She nods at the notebook. "I already know how Pretty In Blue sounds, but what about the other songs? Have you got a score for them?"

I nod after contemplating the questions for a few minutes.

"A few of them," I answer. "I'm still working on the score for most songs. But I have an idea how I want the music to go for most songs. I can make sure I got it all finished for doing studio recordings. There should be enough time for Suzie to learn the music TOO…"

"I'm up for the challenge…" Suzie says, grinning broadly.

"Do you play instruments too, Suzie?" Liz asks.

"I learned to play the violin and I can play a piano," Suzie answers. "And I've tried my hand at drumming too from time to time. It's exhaustive really…"

"I think you playing on a piano will be a good combination with Tash's guitar work…" Liz suggests.

"I'm okay with that," Suzie says. Then she points at the open page in the notebook. "I'm curious about how this song sounds… Play it please? In my mind, when I was reading the lyrics days ago, it sounds melodramatic but I'm guessing you have a different tune for it…"

Chapter Fifteen

The next several hours feel like the happiest time of my life as Liz, Suzie and I sit in Liz's office playing the guitar, singing together and exchanging stories about each other's lives. This time the stories have a happy vibe to them. Suzie and I are awestruck when Liz sings some of her more famous songs for us. We agree that she has true talent and a unique voice only few people can master…

We all glance towards the lift when the familiar sound alerts us that someone has arrived at the floor. A man walks towards us.

"Jake…" Liz calls out. "Come meet my two new friends…"

A tall man with white hair covered over by a purple hat, wearing an over the top leather jacket, jeans and a bright yellow t-shirt under the jacket rushes towards us. He carries a tray with four cups on it.

"Collin said I'd find you up here with your guests," Jake says. "He and his buddies are keeping the idiots at bay…"

Suzie and I glance at one another and frown, confused.

"Collin put them on time out," Jake continues. "They're acting like they may go wherever they want. I suggested to Collin to put them in the rooms in the rafters. It's the best place for them. It's a maze up there and unless you know your way it can take more than an hour to get out from that part of the theatre… I heard you two had a plan for sorting them out. If that's right, it's where you can sort them out. They claim it's haunted up there. An hour alone makes even the toughest guy squeamish and scared like a little kid…"

Suzie and I now smile at one another with conspiratorial, knowing smiles on each of our faces.

"Remember please, I don't want to know what you got planned," Liz hisses at us.

We both nod, agreeing with her, but I already know that Jake, her husband, is the one who'd set the rest of our plan in motion now with some missing information of *how* we'd get our boyfriends up in the rafters where we want to enact our plan. Our devious plan to make them so annoyed with us they'd leave and never want to be around us. Our clever plan to avenge all the wrongs ever done against us. Our plan that would expose their sexual kinks for what they are - a way to exert control over their girlfriends...

"We promise you never know, Liz," we say at the same time with a singsong in our voices.

Jake bursts out laughing when our momentary teasing causes Liz to look annoyed; like we'd ganged up together with Jake to play some prank on her.

Jake walks around the sofa and sits down next to Liz, pulls off his hat for a moment, then he pulls the woman closer and kisses her lips lovingly. Suzie and I glance at one another, smiling. It's obvious to us they genuinely love one another, and while glancing surreptitiously at the two individuals I hope that when I reunite with Tommy that every time he and I are together that we also are as much in love.

Jake places his purple hat back on his head after he has brushed his white hair somewhat excessively with his free hand. I grin when he winks at me and feel surprised when Liz doesn't even react to the obvious flirtation. I think observing these people can teach me about overcoming my doubts about being in love with someone...

+++

Suzie and I sit in front of the window though I don't think where we're sitting is window seating. But as Liz and Jake do the same thing five windows over from us, we stay put. My mind is divided between listening to Suzie's humming, and I appreciate she's helping me with a task that had eluded success for so long and which should cause us sorting out the beginnings of music to go with all the songs, or at least what I thought of as songs, I'd been writing for a decade…

"I never thought I wrote so many songs," I whisper.

"You probably did it to take your mind off the things that happened to you over the years," Suzie whispers back.

"I guess so," I say. "I hope things will go better from now on…"

"They will," Suzie protests. "Especially with Liz and I as your friends, and when you find Tommy…"

"Will I find him? Will I really…?" I ask.

"Of course," Suzie says then glances at her cell phone one more time.

"Can you cut that out?" I ask, feeling annoyed. "Either give me updates on the progress or tell me at the end what the outcome is…"

I frown as Suzie taps her cell phone then she looks up at me, "… Just told her to call me ONLY when she knows where he is and she's found him for definite… Just as you want it…"

"Hmm, I didn't say that," I grunt.

"But you just said that…" Suzie protests.

"I didn't," I grunt.

"Will you really find him…" Suzie mimics my voice teasingly. I glare at her for a moment, then I glance down at the street below. I let my gaze trail over the people walking below us and glance at the nearby buildings.

"For all we know he's somewhere in this city and you were meant to come here to bump into him," Suzie quips.

"I will wait and see if you're right…" I say before I turn my attention back to my notebook and to my effort of deciphering what I'd intended to create with them in terms of words and accompanying music.

It seems Suzie got the message about me wanting to be left alone for a time as she goes silent, and after ten minutes she gets up and moves to the sofa to work on her tasks without distracting me constantly. I glance at her occasionally from the corner of my eye and notice sadness on her face. I glance at the space in front of me for a moment and notice that she's left her cell phone there. I realise that the obsession to find Tommy is consuming her as much as it does me, and that this was a bit of a wake up call to snap her out of her own obsession, if it was that what caused her current behaviour…

+++

I stare in either direction as I stand by the vending machine to make sure I'm not going to get 'pounced' by Mick, who has been strangely absent for most of the afternoon so far. I feel curiosity about what Jake had managed to do to make him behave in this way.

Where is he? I think. *What's he up to?*

I glance in each direction once more, then I listen closely for sounds. It's silent everywhere. Even more so now that most of the crew for the auditions…

I can feel my heart beat, and to my panicked mind it almost sounds like a drumbeat.

Slowly, I walk towards the lift that will lead me back to safety. Liz's office now almost feels like a sanctuary and a place I can just work on my music rather than having to deal with the consequences of my choice of boyfriend.

As I walk, I remember how I had met Mick. He'd been one of those guys who hung around the gigs, not quite part of the crew and not a fan. He had a self-assuredness that had attracted me to him… at first. But slowly over time he'd shown his real self - he was a control freak who would tell the artists how they should do their lighting, performance, eating habits, drinking habits, what girls to date, and he'd get kicked out of bars when he came barging in looking all self-righteous and smug.

He wasn't a knight in shining armour like Tommy had been a few years earlier. Rather than that he picked a fight with the drummer I was sitting next to at the bar, ended up with a black eye and then pulled me with him out of the bar. Somehow I found it attractive for him to do all this in the daze of drunken stupor I was experiencing at the time…

But now…

Now I'm thinking back about, especially after Liz's long story about herself and about the dozens of girls and women she'd pulled from similar situations I wonder seriously *why* I hadn't met Liz in the few months after walking from away Tommy's apartment. Would I have been able to avoid ninety percent of the shit I'd experienced…?

I guess that some books that Suzie says for me to write will be about the shit rather about the nicer things I could write about, I think bitterly. *But maybe doing that will ensure I warn girls from idolising some git on YouTube or allowing someone to be talked into a dangerous situation in a bar…*

Suddenly I realise how different my life was because of one small decision. *Had I stayed with Tommy I could be a successful artist by now? I guess the efforts I'm making now will change all that…*

I sigh, then I press the keypad. Liz had let Suzie and me use her code when it would take many days before a code could be issues to either of us; something to do with checking our IDs and other shit.

Before stepping into the lift, I glance into each direction one more time, then I walk inside. I tap the third button from the top - Liz's office. I fold my arms and wait for the lift to move to its destination. Just thirty seconds later the doors open and I hesitate, walking from the lift. I slam my hand against the door when it closes and grunt with annoyance when pain shoots through my hand. I rush from the lift before it can close a second time.

"FUCK!" I blurt out loudly.

"Are you okay?" Suzie calls out from the corner of the room.
"Yeah, just this damned lift door closed too quickly," I yell back. "I think I bruised my hand somewhat…"
"I hope it's the wrong hand…" Suzie calls out.
"What you mean?" I ask as I walk towards her.
"The hand you need not play the guitar with…"
"Yeah… No… It's okay. The pain is already going away," I grunt as I sit down opposite of her in one chair. "I'm ambidextrous with playing the guitar, though I do it better with this hand." I lift my

left hand. "I hurt my right hand just now…"

"Ah right, you lucky girl…" Suzie quips. "Anyway, I think I figured out a melody for one song… I wrote the notes here…"

Suzie hands me my notebook and I look at the scribbled notes next to my song and in my mind I'm immediately working out how it may sound.

"Play it on the guitar…" Suzie says. "I tried to do it, but I'm not as skilled as you are. It sounded more like I was sawing a plank…"

I lean over the coffee table and take hold of the guitar being held out to me. I place the notebook flat on the table, then read the notes one more time. I check that I tune the guitar, then I play each note. Once I've made myself familiar with all of them, I play them faster in succession, repeating it even faster a moment later.

"I thought of it as a bridge between the third and fourth verse of the song," Suzie suggests. "But a slower version of it."

I nod and repeat the tune a fourth time, but half the speed I'd played it before. I glance up and get a nod of approval. I repeat the faster tune and immediately follow it by the slower bridge, and then I nod too, "I think that will work well…"

"Can you sing the words while you play the tune?" Suzie asks, beaming at me.

"Sure, let me just remember the words first," I answer. I read through the words of my song - called Ladybird - a few times, then I nod one more time.

"I think it will sound best if I use the bridge also as the intro," I suggest, glancing up to determine what Suzie's take is on the idea. She nods enthusiastically.

I play the tune for a long minute before I sing, and when I do I look directly at Suzie. I'll explain later what the significance is of this song. My mind thinks back to the day when I wrote it. It was the morning after I'd argued with my sister. She and I had later met up, and we'd said sorry to one another. She had written the first three lines of the song on her napkin while we drank our coffees. Before leaving, she'd told me to turn the words into a song and for it to teach people about unconditional love.

As I watch tears of happiness stream from Suzie's eyes, something she seems oblivious of, I think I've just fulfilled my sister's wishes…

Chapter Sixteen

Suzie wipes her eyes dry and smiles wistfully, "That was so beautiful…" she whispers. "I love Pretty In Blue but there's something about this song that makes me long for something. I had the feels here…" Suzie taps her upper chest just above her heart. "It sounded like the sort of song that someone might play at a wedding. You wrote it for when you get married to Tommy?"

"No," I answer, looking down for a moment. "My sister wrote part of the words after we'd made up after arguing. She told me to write one line of the song every month on the last day of the month. She told me I had to finish it when I got a contract for a gig…"

"Which you have now…" Suzie comments.

"And she doesn't know," I continue. "She hasn't seen me for a decade… Ever since I hooked up with Mick. He met my Dad and sister once and told me he didn't like them. My sister asked me about him. She said she wasn't sure if he was the right person for me. She doesn't even know about Tommy…"

"What's your sister called?" Suzie asks.

"Brianna," I answer. "She's called after our grandfather Brian…"

"She's older?"

"Yeah, two years older…"

"You said she writes books, right?" Suzie asks as she grabs her phone once more. "So… Brianna McKinsey… Or is she married and writing under that name?"

"Actually, I don't know if she's married…" I admit. "Try Brianna McKinsey. If you can't find her on Amazon, she's might have a pen name or something like that…"

"Half the authors whose books I read are pen names," Suzie

comments. "It's common for them to have a different name. Or even use a few names… What sort of stories did she write?"

"Fantasy… errr… romance… errr… thrillers… or so she claimed to me at least," I answer.

"Romance, huh…" Suzie quips before picking up her bag and tipping the content on the table between us. She spreads the books over the table. "Do you realise that one of these books YOU called ridiculous at first could easily be a book by your sister…?"

Suzie giggles when it's obvious I'm blushing brightly I know I'm blushing because my face feels hot suddenly.

"You made your point," I grunt.

"I guess you'd recognise your sister if you saw a photo of her, right?"

"Of course," I answer.

"Okay then, are any of these ladies your sister?" Suzie asks holding her cell phone in front my face.

I have to squint a few moments to look then I say, "Three of them are not the right skin colour to be her. And unless she's gone blonde two more are not her…"

"Okay, let's check them one by one," Suzie says.

She pulls the phone towards herself and selects a profile then holds the phone towards me again, "Nope…"

"Okay, next one…"

I'm seeing how determined Suzie is as a person because if it had been me I might have given up after just two pages of profiles of authors, many of whom I'd never heard of and I realise now how few romance novels I'd read. I end up admitting to myself that the novels I borrowed from Suzie were actually the first ones I read. To discover that the very genre of stories I never had been reading COULD be the very genre where I might find my sister, or should I say rediscover her, came as a shock to me…

"That's her," I blurt out when Suzie holds up her phone again.

"So she writes as Brianna Kinsey… hmm, interesting…" Suzie comments as she stares at the profile. "I can understand why she did that. It creates a bit of anonymity that way. Let's see…"

I wait for Suzie to look over the page.

"She has three books out," Suzie says, looking up at me. "Two are romance, the third is a fantasy novel about dragons. It says here she has another pen name…”

"Are you sure you're not like your friend?” I ask.

"What? You mean my Polish friend… Naah, I'd be bored stiff doing her line of work,” Suzie says.

"Yet you're doing it now,” I say then I topple backwards in my chair laughing so loudly that I snort in the middle of it. "Private—Sextective—Suzie…” I snort.

"Sextective…?” Suzie asks.

"Yeah, a detective who solves sleuth stuff using sex as a weapon…” I reply then I coo at her, "Miiiick… Timooothy…”

"Ooh right…” Suzie says then she's laughing as hard as I am. "Okay, Sextective Suzie is on the case to find your sister… She has a website… And she's on Facebook…”

I jerk up, "She is… She always claimed she hated it…”

I grab my phone, "Send me a message with her details…

"Sure…”

"Do you mind if I'm going to the other end of the office to see if I can get hold of her?” I ask.

"Of course not,” Suzie answers. "I might be an only child but I got cousins with siblings and can see how much of a bond they got between them… Actually, I'll go. I can keep Liz and Jake from here if they come back. Mind if I take a few notebooks with me to work with?”

"Go ahead,” I answer.

I glance after Suzie, feeling grateful now. Up to now I'd still doubted her sincerity about finding Tommy, but her quick effort of tracking down my sister changed everything…

I dial the number I'd written from Facebook and I wait a few minutes. Someone answers the phone after four rings and a familiar voice answers the phone…

"Hi, Brianna, it's me…”

It's silent for several minutes, and for a moment, I think either I had the wrong person, or she'd hung up on me…

"Tash, oh my god, Tash, where HAVE you been all these years?” Brianna shrieks. "I've missed you SO very much… WHERE are you? How are you? Are you singing still? How are you? I missed you, sis…"

It takes several minutes of Brianna shrieking over the phone before I can get a word in, "I'm fine. I'm actually waiting for the outcome of an audition I was in…"

"Where?" Brianna asks.

"In London…" I answer.

"How the hell did you get over there…?" Brianna asks. "The last I heard you were… errr… I got told you were in New York or even San Francisco…"

"I flew to London six months ago…" I explain. I omit Mick's existence, seeing as I was hoping to get things sorted out again with Tommy.

"Are you okay though? Do you need any money?" Brianna asks.

"Nooo, I'm fine…" I answer. "And if the audition doesn't work out, I'm likely landing a contract with Liz James… Yes that Liz James, married to Jake, who's been a singer for over two decades…"

"Wow, I've heard about her…" Brianna blurts out. "She's famous as hell. From what I know of her she's got her own label and recording studio…"

My eyes widen with surprise. Now it made sense why Liz COULD offer us a deal of her own if the deal from the auditions didn't happen.

"Errr… Brianna… I need to mute you a moment, please," I say.

"Okay."

I mute the cell phone and yell loudly, "Liz James apparently has a label and a recording studio. Go Sextective with that, will ya… I'm still talking to my sis…"

"Okay, back," I say as Suzie's voice yells out, "What the effing fuck…"

"Who's that?" Brianna asks.

"My band mate…" I answer. "She's called Suzie."

"That would be Sextective Suzie, thank you very much, Miss Know-It-All," Suzie yells back at me before laughing hysterically.

"She sounds like a fun person," Brianna says. "Any chance I can meet her one day?"

"Sure," I answer. "We're in London. Where do you live these days?"

"I'm on a book tour in Paris…" Brianna says. "If you found me by looking up books, you must have seen my latest book on

Amazon…"

"Yeah, I did," I answer. "I think Suzie bought all your books by now…"

"And I did the same for you," Suzie yells from across the office.

"And apparently, I'll get one of each of your books, too," I add to the obvious comment that's overheard by Brianna based on her momentary snickering.

"When I'm back in England we should meet up," Brianna says. "Bring your friend, your band mate too. I'd love to get to know her."

"I might have others to bring along too but that's not yet confirmed," I say and for a moment I expect Suzie to yell out about Tommy but this time she's conspicuously quiet. "We'll sort out the details later on, okay?"

"Sure thing," Brianna says.

Suddenly, I feel the urge to broach the topic that had weighed heavy my mind over the last few years and I ask hesitantly, "How's Dad?"

"He misses you. He talks all the time about you and was wondering where you'd ended up…" Brianna mumbles. "I must tell him you called me. I would call him later this evening. I'll tell him you called from a pay phone so he doesn't demand to have your cell phone number."

"I feel awkward about losing touch with both of you," I say. "I hope you forgive me…"

"Naah, we're sisters. There's nothing to forgive…" Brianna says.

"I finished Ladybird," I blurt out. "We even have a nice melody for it…"

"You got a talented sister, do you hear me…" Suzie yells from across the room.

"When you visit, you can sing it to me…" Brianna says, laughing.

"You will. I promise," I say.

"I got to go now, sis. They need me for a book signing…" Brianna breathes. "Talk to you soon again, okay? And NOT in ten years from now…"

"I'll call you this evening…" I promise.

+++

After another twenty minutes of us working on a few more of the songs and determining any possible music to go with them, Suzie sits upright suddenly and places the two notebooks she was reading through to one side.

She stares at me resolutely.

"What?" I ask, annoyed.

"Did you forget something?" Suzie quips. "Such as... two annoying guys..."

"I didn't, actually. When I went to get a drink, I got paranoid about Mick being somewhere nearby and watching me all the time," I blurt out.

"But I thought they were being guarded by Jake's guys?" Suzie asks.

"I think they were because there wasn't anyone anywhere."

"So why are you paranoid then?" Suzie asks, frowning somewhat.

"I don't know. I just was, okay," I answer. "Now either shut up about it or are we doing something about it..."

"Well..." Suzie says conspiratorially.

"Well, what?"

"We have to go NOW... While they're gone, Tash," Suzie whispers, although I'm unsure why she sees the need to whisper as we're alone and not likely to be heard outside Liz's office. "We need to get this done and dusted BEFORE Liz and Jake come back from the shop. So we can deal with those loser boyfriends, and so we can start afresh afterwards and all that shit, and then go on to the next step of us finding Tommy... And I'll shut up about him too before you tell me to shut up..."

I glance around and realise now why Suzie suggested.

I had forgotten for a while we're alone...

+++

We rush through the theatre towards the rafters, and glance surprise towards one another when on one end of the corridor Timothy sits sulking, and the other side it's Mick tapping ferociously on his cell phone. We step back so we're not spotted immediately.

"Jake said there were several corridors," Suzie whispers. "He said that you can reach Mick via another small corridor further along. You get him in place, then come back here, and then you go sort out Timothy. Once you're gone I'll go to Mick… You're still up for the plan, right?"

I nod.

"Okay then, go now…" Suzie whispers.

"Break a leg," Suzie gently calls out after me.

I turn and I give her an odd glance for a moment then I realise what she's eluding at with the comment and then I also realise that the next hour I'd be doing what could essentially our first, and only, acting role. I suddenly hope that was the case. And the outcome of all this nonsense - a new life and a chance at proper happiness…

+++

Glancing sideways towards Mick, I contemplate how to put the plan that Suzie and I'd been discussing for the better part of the day, into action without him realising I'm playing him for a fool "Put on this blindfold," I whisper teasingly into Mick's ear. "I have a surprise for you…"

Immediately, Mick's hand lifts up and it's quickly under my top, rubbing my skin. I let him do this for a few minutes before I push his hand away abruptly, and I step back. I have a different plan in mind compared to what I told him to surprise him. Mick was about to find out how…

Chapter Seventeen

Mick glances at me surprised for several minutes, then he smirks when he sees my hand pull up my skirt. He reaches for my leg but I push his hand away, and I say alluringly, "Not yet. First the blindfold…"

I hold up the rag that Suzie had found in the prop room downstairs. Mick frowns and appears like he wants to get up and walk away. I grab his arm and look at him imploringly, "You asked me earlier if there was any kink I wanted to do while we were here. I've decided on one kink I've wanted to do forever…"

I glance sidelong towards the doorway and I hope that Suzie is waiting to walk into the room. If I could consider this dusty cupboard a room at all. I put my face neutral when I glance back towards Mick, and I have to suppress a smile when I see him fastening the blindfold obligingly. I'm guessing that he's going along with my suggested kink.

"Okay, so now what?" Mick grunts. I grin broadly now that he's unable to see my reactions. I suppress my giggling when I see him reach out like he's trying to make sure he doesn't stumble over some theatre props lying on the surrounding floor. I get up quietly and step over the props and reach for his hand. He flinches when I touch his hand…

"What's the matter?" I ask. "Did I scare you?"
"Not sure if I like this…" Mick grunts.

"Why not?" I ask. "I thought you wanted to do some of my kinks because they sounded interesting to you…"

"I don't feel secure doing it here with all this mess around us…" Mick grunts.

"Just sit down on the padding behind you," I suggest. "I'll make you comfortable…"

Mick reaches behind him while I gently push him. After a minute he flops down on the padding and after feeling beside him for several minutes he folds his arms and looks towards me guessing where I might be standing. I step back a few paces to make sure he can't do the obvious 'thing' he'd usually do whenever I stand in front of him and when he wants to exert his 'dominance' over me in our supposed relationship.

A moment later he reaches out with the obvious intent to do exactly that action.

Yeah, a supposed relationship, I think bitterly. I feel my face contort with bitterness. *I guess he's totally forgotten about our argument last week. I did too, to be honest. I guess that goes with this unconventional lifestyle as he wants to have with me. Suzie was right…*

I check over my shoulder because now I wonder if Suzie is as successful with fooling her boyfriend into a similar compromised situation. I hear someone cough in the distance. I'm guessing it's Suzie.

"Who coughed…?"

I jerk my head around because Mick's voice sounded almost like a squeal of a boy half his age. I smirk with delight as it meant I had made him uncomfortable. I think this is the first time in his life Mick is at someone else's mercy. My mercy…

"I think it came from downstairs," I whisper. "Not sure where from exactly. I will check…"

I decided this is a perfect moment for me to leave the room and find Suzie and for her to end up here in my place. She'd shown me where her boyfriend would be so I could rush there quickly. I stop at the doorway and stare back at Mick who sits on the padding and from time to time reaches around him with a stretched out arm.

He assumes I'd stay here with him. What a fool...

+++

Suzie is waiting for me at the bottom of the stairs and when I reach her she glances up and she whispers, "Does he actually *know* what's going on?"

I shake my head and reply affirmatively, "He's in the dark about what we're doing..."

"My idiot is never clued up about what's going on..." Suzie quips. "He's dutifully sitting in the room at the end of the downstairs corridor—You know where the dressing rooms are in this hellhole, right?"

"I had a bit of an issue finding them when I arrived but yes, I know where they are," I answer. "My room is the second on the right downstairs."

"Ah, that means we're side by side," Suzie says, grinning. "I'm in room three..."

We both glance up when Mick's familiar voice calls out, "Tash, where are you?"

"Just talking to one caretaker..." I call out. "He wants to know about my rig setup..."

"Just hurry... I don't feel safe with this blindfold on," Mick calls back.

"Is he always this squeamish?" Suzie whispers. "If so, I'll have a lot of fun teasing him soon. Are you ready to do your part?"

I nod.

"You're sure your skills of acting are ace so we can to succeed with this—" Suzie says. I interrupt her bluntly, "—with this scheme of making our boyfriends cheat on us without them knowing it. Yeah, yeah, I know what I need to do. It was obvious what I need to do based on how he reacted towards me up there..."

I motion towards the stairway and where the sounds of Mick's whimpering are coming from.

Suzie looks up to the top of the stairs for a moment then back at me then adds, "I guess I should get in action before he becomes suspicious..."

"Have fun," I say sarcastically. "I think he believed me when I said it's one of my kinks..."

"It's not?" Suzie asks.

I shake my head. Up to when Mick had put on the blindfold, I thought it was a kink I would have enjoyed. But when his hand reached out for my leg, and therefore also tried to push his hand up under my skirt, the feeling of superiority had evaporated fast…

I tuck clumsily at the edge of my skirt. Suddenly feeling subconscious about the earlier encounter between Suzie and myself, I feel shy about wearing a short skirt.

I guess it will wear trousers from now on whenever I go out, but even then I could be vulnerable. I guess I understand now whenever someone in the industry talks about the culture of industry…

"Are you okay?" Suzie asks.

"No, actually…" I answer bluntly. "I'm annoyed about what you did earlier. And now you come up with this shit…"

"I'm sorry I had to do that…" Suzie says glumly. "I had to be sure…"

"Sure with what, huh?" I snap. "With me being treated like a whore or something like that?"

"Actually, it's the opposite…" Suzie says apologetically.

"In what way?" I ask.

"Didn't you say you wanted your old boyfriend back?"

I nod curtly then stare up the stairway for a while thinking about the scheme Suzie had dreamt up. I nod again after a few minutes and, looking again at Suzie, I say, "Go ahead, I guess he's awaiting his kink…"

Suzie smiles then says, "I'll make it worth your while. He'll be so embarrassed when he comes to find you later that it will be easy for you to tell him you had enough of him…"

"I'll do the same with Timothy, I guess…" I suggest. "Except, I guess, I'm teaching him that being a prude is as stupid as being obsessed with sex like my loser boyfriend seems to be…"

"It's hilarious to realise how different they can both be—" I continue. "I have an oversexed boyfriend… Is undersexed even a word? If so, that's your boyfriend's problem. I'm guessing that a decade from now we'll be sitting in some cafeteria laughing and joking about this. But right now it feels weird, annoying and disgusting to me to even having to do this stuff…"

"But if the friend I called earlier is successful, you'll have something better to look forward to," Suzie quips. "She's very good at finding people…"

"I hope so…" I say. "I doubt I could look Mick in the eyes after THIS…"

"Shh…" Suzie says, placing a hand over my lips. "Don't want him to hear you…"

I nod profusely.

After a few minutes' silence, both of us listening to the grunts and mumbling coming from the storage room above us, we stare at one another with an equal cheeky grin plastered on our faces. Although I've always been straight, suddenly, I felt an ounce of attraction for Suzie. She's a beautiful woman with a sculpted appearance and a smoothness in her facial features that could easily get her a contract as a model for a magazine. For a minute, I feel an attraction and feel the urge to return the favour of what had occurred between us in the restroom. I inch closer…

When I'm close up to Suzie, I stare down at her. I didn't realise up that moment that the corridor was slightly sloped. As I closed in I realise now that I'm just a few inches taller than she is. I lean in, and before she can do anything in protest, I kiss her on her lips. I feel surprise when I get a response to my actions. She pushes closer against me too. My tongue probes her parted lips. I may not be a lesbian but my second lesbian encounter with Suzie proves that she and I felt similar for one another in feeling attraction to one another…

I feel her stiffen up as much as I'd done earlier when my hand finds its way inside her jeans and a finger inserts into her pussy. I don't think she'd counted on THIS being my kink: sex with a girl in a dark corridor. Or… as close as I could be to the kink under the circumstances. I may not be a lesbian, but it doesn't stop me having kinks that are essentially lesbian in nature…

After a few minutes I push Suzie away from me with my free hand and stare at her grinning broadly then I ask, "Did you expect this from me?"

Suzie shakes her head, then closes her eyes as I rub her pussy faster and harder.

"He'll be pleased if you're already turned on…" I whisper. "I usually have to do this before I get in bed with him. He will expect a ready wet pussy…"

"It—it feels so—good," Suzie moans softly. My response to the compliment is to rub her clit even harder, and to probe her pussy even deeper with my finger. I may not be a lesbian, but this feels good to me too. Suzie tries to kiss me again. To my surprise, I let her do it. Her hand finds my boob and squeezes it and then her other hand has found its way into my panties, and her hand is again rubbing my clit as much as I'm doing the same to her. I moan, too…

That Suzie and I are having full on lesbian sex just yards from Mick who's sitting blindfolded is turning me on even more than before. But as Suzie said moments earlier, we have goals to achieve here. As abruptly as I'd begun with the sexual encounter between us, I end it. I step away, then nod towards the stairway…

Suzie nods, and without saying a word to me, she ascends the stairs. I listen for whatever might happen next. I grin broadly once more when I hear Suzie talking. She's doing a damned good imitation of my voice and speech patterns. It proves she's right about one thing: she's a damned good actress. Perhaps that's another asset in our upcoming arsenal as the Rose Petals. And who knows? Maybe the dream of being an actress one day could also still be on the cards if my own actions can persuade Timothy that I'm Suzie…

I walk away quietly in the direction that Suzie had arrived from. I open a door and find myself staring at the sort of man I would have wished for as a boyfriend. Her prude boyfriend is easily mistaken for a model from a magazine cover.

"Hi there…" I say teasingly.

"Who are you?" Timothy asks.

"I didn't expect anyone to be here," I say, knowing full well that it's a lie. "I was looking for somewhere to practise my role in a movie they cast me for…"

"Oh, what role?" Timothy asks. I see him eyeing me all over, and it's obvious he's judging me for appearance and possible abilities.

"It's rather embarrassing…"

"How?" he asks.

"Because… errr… because it involves a sex scene with a guy…" Feigning reluctance, I pretend to be shy to gain his possible trust. "I would act out the part where I seduce him… but… errr…"

"Am I in the way?" he asks.

"No, actually. I was wondering if you could help me with it…"

Chapter Eighteen

If Timothy is some sort of a prude, it isn't showing in his actions right now. He's so eager to participate in the 'audition' of a supposed sex scene from a non-existent movie that I suggested is a big secret of some sort. He's eager to hold my boobs, and to lean against my ass with his dick that's getting stiff really fast.

I'm thinking he's just with the *wrong* woman…

"In the movie I'm supposed to undress myself," I say glancing back at Timothy. "I want to feel comfortable doing this in front of a studio of people who I don't even know. So, if I feel okay doing it in front of you, then I'm certain I'll be able to do it later in front of all of them…"

Timothy nods, and I notice a cheeky grin play over his lips. It seems he wants this stuff to happen. I slowly inch closer to him to see how he reacts to being so close to me. His smile widens, especially when my hands take hold of the first button of my skirt. He pulls me closer to him, ever so gently, by holding a button. I don't resist his actions. Not yet, at least…

He seems eager to play out some fantasy of his own, and now I realise how correct Suzie's assessments are of how he'd behave with me, and how different I compare him to what Suzie had told me about his behaviour towards her. It amuses me to see him squirm from wanting to have his ways with me and his loyalty, misplaced or otherwise, towards Suzie…

No wonder she's gone off him, smirking when my head leans on Timothy's shoulder.

At first he seems eager with touching my body, but at a few minutes he hesitates more and more, and then after fifteen minutes he has completely stopped his behaviour. This isn't the behaviour to get to the climax of this weird sex story going on between Suzie and me with us doing some sort of revenge act on our boyfriends…

"Why did you stop…?" I ask. "The scene in the movie is much longer than this… I need to cope with several takes…"

"I don't know why I stopped," Timothy answers, sounding glum and almost like he's annoyed. "I guess I never knew until now that I wouldn't like this fantasy…"

I do my best not to burst out in laughter at the response. I'm guessing already that the response would make Suzie laugh too. It's NOT the response of someone who had, apparently, taunted his girlfriend for weeks to do some boyfriend swap with someone…

I do my best not to burst out in laughter at the response. I'm guessing already that the response would make Suzie laugh too. It's NOT the response of someone who had, apparently, taunted his girlfriend for weeks with the idea of doing some sort of boyfriend swap with someone…

I decide to mess with his mind, asking, "Don't you like how I look?"

"No, no, no, you're gorgeous," Timothy answers hastily. "I guess if I'd met you before… errr… Well, I guess I'm realising now I was way too soon with settling with one person…"

"You—have—a—girlfriend," I gasp, pretending to be offended by his admission.

Timothy blushes. Even in the dim light of where we are, I can see him go bright red in the face. I realise suddenly what I can do to change the situation I find myself in. I go through my mind for every acting skill I've ever learned in the last decade and set about to do my damnedest to make Timothy so uncomfortable that he won't stick around when he discovers that Suzie and I are friends.

Suddenly I feel like something has changed, *Suzie is a friend. For real?*

Now I realise what she suggested about this situation. I didn't need to go as far as having sex with this loser and only pretend I would do it to make him unsettled., Suzie and I were acting out some revenge scene from one of Suzie's collection of sleazy novels I had been reading over the last few days that, as Suzie suggested, would give me ideas for what I need to do…

I can do something like that girl in the last book I read, I think. She got the guy turned on before she screwed him over royally with leaving him alone naked. Add some of Mick's kinks to the mix and I got a cure for Timothy to put him off girls for life…

I'm surprised when having sex with someone I don't even know seems to turn me on so incredibly. Never had Mick's kinks turned me on, but now with this guy they do…

+++

Feeling emboldened, I grin delighted when another crazy idea comes to my mind that either I could remove Timothy's clothing OR that I could convince him to remove his own clothing. It might be a lot easier to convince him of my imaginary scene that I lifted from one books I read. Such as the book by the American author that I finished just this morning might suit my needs. I think for a moment then I walk back towards Timothy…

I look him over to determine what I can do first, and I think about the doubts I feel. *Also, how far I should go. Also, how much will keep me comfortable? How much of what I'm doing will haunt me in the years to come? Am I doing the right thing?*

I had only unbuttoned my top a little so far, but I now I was determined to take things a step further. I reach up and unbutton my top further. I can see his eyes glued on my chest, wanting to see what's in store for him. It's obvious now that he lusts for what I'm offering him. The possibility of me wanting to have sex with him obviously…

Timothy grabs my hand when I reach down to lift my top over my head and stops me in mid-action and he asks me, "Do you want to do this?"

I think for a moment, then I nod resolutely and I remove my top in a quick motion. I stand in front of Timothy, and now I only wear my skirt, underwear and bra. Timothy's hand now caresses the skin of my belly, never going near my boobs or my skirt. It surprises me he wouldn't touch me. Maybe he's feeling as insecure as I feel right now. I make my body rigid so not to make him realise this about me, or realise that I'm noticing the same about him…

If I'm right about him, I think before I grab hold of his hand. Now I'm indecisive about to do next. He seems to want to stop the indecisiveness that had stalled our 'game' so when he reaches for the button on my skirt - not that it seems much of a skirt based on previous events - I just let him get on with it and unbutton it and pull down the zip. He seems to wait a moment then he tugs at my skirt to pull it down over my hips but he stops when my skirt is only an inch or so lower than it usually would be.

Now Timothy's hands caress again over the skin of belly, but then one hand rises towards my boob. It pauses a moment, then he reaches for my right boob and slides his hand under my bra. I hold my breath in anticipation what he may do next. The sensation of someone else's hand caressing my body feels rather odd to me suddenly, but it's nice at the same time.

"Your skin is so soft, do you know that," Timothy whispers. "I normally don't do this…"

But you do, I think. *Your behaviour right now tells me you cheat all the time. I guess that's why Suzie wants rid of you…*

I keep my gaze neutral - so I don't give away, I'm more aware of what's going on than he realises. I've finally figured out what Suzie had been trying to tell me for several days - she wants to be alone, single, uncommitted or whatever because of how this guy is behaving when presented by temptation. It's laughable when I realise I'm doing the exact same thing. But I left him when I walked away from Mick after we had sex. I've already dumped him…

"Your hand is still on my boob," I quip teasingly. "I guess this isn't normally..."

Timothy cocks his head back in surprise, but he doesn't take his hand away. His other hands covers my other boob a moment later. It's obvious now what he wants from me and from this moment.

+++

Without warning, I grab hold of his shirt and I quickly unbutton the rest of it. He stares surprised at me for a moment then he grabs my hand to stop me but not long after it he lowers his hand and he seems to wait for what I might do next. I unbutton his shirt two times more and stare at his smooth chest. Comparing him now to Mick with his very hairy chest makes me flutter with a feeling I'd last felt years ago when I had been with... Tommy.

For a moment I want to push away from Timothy because my mind had turned to remembering Tommy and to the last few days spent with him. Lovemaking had always been intense between Tommy and me, so I quickly replace this memory with the content of the conversation I had with Suzie and what she'd said about me getting naked. I decide that I need to pretend Timothy is some assistant at a concert and NOT Suzie's supposed boyfriend. Without Timothy noticing, I shake my head to dispel the dark thought had entered my mind.

I dismiss ever finding Tommy for a moment and continue unbuttoning Timothy's shirt. After another minute he sits with his chest showing, and he shows a pleased grin at the possibilities this moment was creating. I swallow hard. Part of me wants to just walk away, but the chance of having some fun now excited another part of me.

I run my finger over Timothy's chest, smiling at him at the same time. I force myself to continue my actions when he runs the back of his hand over my cheek. Then suddenly he grabs hold of me and pulls me close to him. I feel awkward about being naked already, but suddenly I want him. Suddenly I lust for Timothy with no reservation. It scares me, yet I feel empowered by these new feelings soaring through my body.

Now I wonder how far I want to take things with Timothy. Would I dare to have sex with him? Suzie's idea had been that we just tease each of our loser boyfriends, but a small part of me tries to imagine intercourse with him.

"Do you want to do this?" he asks.

"Yes, I want it…" I whisper back. "Please, fuck me…"

Suddenly, now there's the idea that I'd given him consent, there's urgency in Timothy's actions as he yanks down my skirt and a moment later a few fumbling fingers have removed my bra. I'm surprised that I'm not shocked by standing naked. Timothy stands to his feet and quickly unbuttons his trousers. He grabs me by my waist and lifts me on the pile of wood covered by a thick curtain, then he leans in and kisses my lips hard. He pushes me gently to my back and leans down and suck each of my nipples for several minutes. I can feel his dick harden against my leg and it causes me to move my legs apart. He glances at me with a smirk, then he pushes. He enters my pussy cleanly and deep. I gasp…

I expect him to penetrate me hard, but he's slow and makes it feel good. Very good…

Another gasp when he re-enters me. Slowly, he speeds until he's pumping fast. He groans loud when he explodes inside me. He pushes inside me, pauses and holds his dick inside my pussy for long enough for it to give me one more orgasm, then he pulls out and flips his dick against my clit a few times. Then he's gone, and I find out a kink I'm sure that Suzie doesn't know about. Or at least, she's not said anything about it.

I gasp when Timothy flicks his tongue over my clit fast and really thoroughly. He holds my hands tightly beside my body, so when I squirm under the pleasuring, I cannot move away. Whatever I do, I'm pinned down and subjected to his licking until I pant loudly and arch my body in response. I've never had sex like this with anyone, not even Tommy…

The thought of Tommy pulls me out of the moment, and I free my hands and push his head away. I scramble upright and stare at Timothy standing a few feet from me, looking glum and defeated. I grin when I see his dick flaccid.

"My turn," I quip teasingly.

Chapter Nineteen

After unexpectedly getting a few minutes of sex with a man I don't know I get up and I decide to try out another kink of Mick's so I ask, "Want to do something kinkier than all this sex…?" adding a moment later, "I need to do something for this kink but you'll have to trust me…"

Timothy nods and I walk around the room for what I need. The cool breeze from somewhere tells me that this part of the building had no heating. It would get cold here, but now I don't care about the consequences. Suddenly, I don't feel comfortable going through with what I had wanted to do when I first had unbuttoned his shirt…

I stare at Timothy lying passively on his back and I'm bemused when he even lets me tie his hands with two pieces of rope. But by now I have no intention of going through with this sex game he wants. If Suzie can do the same with Mick she and I got exactly what we wanted from this plan - the utter humiliation when the caretaker, or whoever cleans up around here in the rafters of the theatre, finds each of them.

I turn, dress myself, and ignoring the calls of protest yelled at me by Timothy as I quickly walk away from him. As my step hastens, I just hope the future involves Tommy. I hope that Suzie's friend finds him and soon.

A final glance back at a squirming Timothy who's trying to

dislodge my handiwork of tying him up; a skill learned from Mick of all people. I turn and rush down several flights of stairs to get back to the green room where Suzie and I would regroup…

+++

I sit down at the bottom of the second staircase and contemplate about everything that had happened in the last hour. I think back to the conversation earlier between Liz, Suzie and myself. I had answered in the negative when confronted with the question about whether I wanted to see Tommy again…

I reach for my bag I'd left on the stairs when I went up to the rafters with Timothy. I reach in the side pocket for my 'emergency package.' From it I grab a box of pills. My morning-after pills in case I ended up sleeping somewhere in the streets. But now, the emergency is to prevent a new mistake from entering my life. I didn't want to find Tommy, only to discover I got pregnant by either of the guys I'd slept with in the last few days. It wasn't the first time I had casual sex with a guy. Often enough I'd ended up sleeping with someone after taking part in some gig as a backup singer to give me the money for the bus fare to the next town on my trek to whatever my end destination might be in my effort to escape from a past that - up to now - I'd always regarded as miserable and annoying…

But it was the best time of my life, I think. *Why the fuck did I ever leave Tommy? Would he even want me back? Has he been searching for me? Will he forgive me?*

Memories of Tommy come flooding into my mind and they drown out the calls of protest still emerging from time to time from above me where obviously Timothy is finding it tough to escape the bondage contraption I had fastened him in. I guess certain things learned from my life with Mick, as well all his nasty cronies, was coming in handy right now. I glance up once, then move down to the next staircase to lessen the impact of his calls on my little attempt of going down the memory lane.

I grab the latest book borrowed from Suzie, which I'd been reading while she was in her audition. It's the story of these two people meeting one another by chance and then organising a road trip together. I hope Suzie will forgive me for giving the book a dog-ear of the chapter that had started my memories of Tommy. In this chapter, the guy found the girl, and I had wiped away a tear.

Yeah, yeah, Tash... Sometimes these stupid books have a good story. Maybe now work on your own happy ending with Tommy. Maybe start believing that I can find him and that he wants you back. Sometimes you should listen to good advice when it's thrown in your face...

Hoisting myself to my feet, I suddenly feel like I have a new mission ahead - the mission that involves Tommy. I lift my cell phone from my bag and glance through the list of phone numbers there in the hopes I've not been as stupid as I suddenly feel...

Nope, his phone number isn't there...

I check my voice messages just in case he left me a voice message I hadn't deleted yet.

No voice messages... Dammit, girl, you remember why they're gone...

I check the text message with no good outcome.

"I guess I must confront Suzie about her damned friend," I mumble under my breath while I glance around me to decide what to do next. "Maybe I just have to confront the inevitable and just deal with her loser boyfriend for a little longer... Dammit, dammit, dammit—"

I stop my incessant monologue when I hear Timothy call out with anger in his voice, and now sounding somewhat menacing and explaining by his attitude why Suzie wants to be rid of him, "... You know I CAN hear every word you just said, you stupid bitch. I'll teach you a lesson when I get out of this reenactment from filthy shades..."

"Ha, you don't even know the name of the damned book or movie, you stupid bitch," I blurt out loudly then I turn, grab my bag and rush through the corridor to the other end of the rafters and make sure I'm out of sight just in case Timothy untangles himself from my five minutes of indulging in Mick's kink of bondage and that shit.

I find myself slumped in a chair, breathing fast and feeling somewhat afraid now of what I'd done. I'm certain I could be safely away from Timothy if I give myself a chance to figure out the layout of the theatre. The safest place would be Liz's office but I didn't know the code yet - she was sorting out one for each of Suzie and me but we'd have the details tomorrow. And she'd gone home already…

Maybe I should just go back to the green room, which I can latch from the inside, and wait there until it's time for me to meet up with Suzie. In case there's something she never told me about Timothy.

I rush now through the corridor to a door I know leads to the auditorium, and after looking for five minutes to check if Mick, as an idiot, was napping there somewhere I slam the door shut, lean against it and I'm panting like I'd just ran to a train station because I'm late for the train…

My panic attack overwhelms me for a moment, then I walk onward. I want to ensure that I'm safe instead of finding myself in a situation similar to all the times when I'd been at gigs. Safety means somewhere that Timothy won't find me. Because of how I'm now feeling, I stop caring about finding out whatever Suzie is doing with Mick. I just want to get safe and for the day to be over and done with… well, at least except for the part where I'd be rushing into Tommy's arms…

+++

It seems to take me longer to arrive at the green room than it had done earlier in the day. While I walk there, I go over the way the day has gone…

A moment later I hear someone running and yell out, "I guess that bitch left…"

I jerk to a halt when I hear an outer door slam shut in the distance and I stand frozen in place for several minutes.

Silence…

I walk to one window and stare down to the street. I giggle when I see Timothy rushing away from the theatre. Stomping like he's in a bad mood…

Suzie will be happy that he's definitely gone, I think.

I recall what Liz had said before she'd left for the shops with Jake, "Don't leave the theatre because if you go outside you're locked out from the building. You'd have to wait for me to let you back in…"

As I watch Timothy disappearing fast along the busy road, my panic also lessens quickly. I'm guessing that he wanted to check if I was outside, but then found himself locked out. I'm guessing he's now walking to whatever hotel Suzie and he is staying in with the hopes she might be there and able to fix it he can get back inside the theatre.

I wonder how the hell he'd try to explain why he has to come back inside. It's not like he was in the audition or shit like that. If he locked in any bags, that's his own fault. He'll just have to come back tomorrow to get them. Tomorrow I'll go away with Suzie…

I glance around the city vista. Something I hadn't really done up to now. I gaze for several minutes at a building opposite of the theatre and after a few minutes I decide its butt ugly and out-of-place even though something about it feels familiar to me knowing why.

I pick up my bag from the floor a moment later and walk through the corridor to the stairs that will lead me to the green room. As I walk, I hope that Mick goes soon too so that Suzie and can continue our work…

I stop again when from ahead of me I hear two people laughing and after a few minutes I grumble under my breath, "Okay, so Liz and Jake are now back. I guess she'll be annoyed we're gone from the office, but I guess she'll understand we can't keep working without breaks. I hope she thinks we've gone for something to eat in the cafeteria even if it's just junk food from the vending machines…"

Curiosity overwhelms me and I rush towards their voices come from, casting one final glances over the square and then thinking, *That ugly building doesn't belong here…*

Once I reach the furthest staircase I'm met by a surprised Liz and Jake who glance at one another then back at me. "What's wrong, Tash?" Liz asks immediately.

"Nothing. Suzie and I just needed food, so we went to the cafeteria to raid the vending machine, or more precise I did. Not sure where Suzie is right now. She might have gone to the restroom," I answer and sincerely hope I'm believed. I glance behind me like I'm searching for Suzie.

"Was that her friend I saw leaving just now?" Jake asks. He makes it obvious he knows what each of our so-called boyfriends looks like. "Where's that loser calling himself your boyfriend…?"

I jerk my gaze back to the couple and shrug my shoulders, "Not seen him since before the auditions. He's probably exploring now everyone is gone. He does that thing whenever we're at some theatre somewhere."

I cringe when Jake pulls out his cell phone, dials a number and talks to one of the two caretakers from earlier. After a nod, he ends the call and puts the cell phone away, "Collin will look for him and expel him from the building. Only the staff, Liz, me, you and Suzie are authorised to be here right now…"

"Let's go back to my office and wait there for Suzie," Liz says.

With Liz and Jake ahead of me, I grab my phone and text Suzie to warn her of the impending discovery of her with Mick if they were still up in the rafters. I breathe a sigh of relief when Suzie texts me back with the news that she was in the restroom beside the cafeteria and that 'the loser has left the building.'

I quickly text Suzie letting her know where to go now, then rush to catch up with Liz and Jake as they've reached the lift to her offices. We're all silent inside the lift, and when you get to the floor with the office, Liz places the four bags she carries on the desk, and Jake places the four bags he carries on the coffee table.

"We didn't know if you had food or not so we bought enough food in case you two would want some," Jake says, grinning at me then flashing me a wink when I look up at him, distracted from texting Suzie. I feel my cheeks go hot and I'm certain he made me blush.

"Stop teasing the poor girl," Liz calls out.
"I only winked at her, love," Jake snorts.
"If you knew more of what happened to her, you'd give her a bit of peace," Liz says in a mock-accusing voice.
"It's okay, Liz," I say. "I've had worse than winks. Someone as nice as Jake can wink at me…"

Chapter Twenty

Once I sit on the sofa I had wondered if Suzie was going to wait at the green room for me. This plan changed because I grouped up with Liz and Jake. I'd sat for the longest time on the final staircase considering all my option, even risking the ridicule from Timothy when he said he heard me talking. I was certain that Suzie was going to charm Mick with the promise of sex in much the same way as I'd done, and as I stare at a blank page of one of the notebooks leaning against my lifted legs I suddenly realise that I didn't care about it.

No more stupidity from Mick if he has really left. I feel a weight come off my shoulders for the first time in many months. *He's gone now…*

I grab my cell phone and I flip through the address book listings. I pull up Mick's number. After a pause, I click on the button at the top right that allows me to block the number from dialling my phone. I deleted the number from the list. I go to the Facebook app, and I block him over there too. I flip through the list of contacts and delete any person I know is his friend. Slowly, I erase him from my existence…

I know Liz is watching my actions. Obviously, curious about it but too polite - I think - to ask me. I can see a knowing, almost fatherly stare from Jake from the corner of my eye a moment after. I glance passes between Liz and Jake. I realise they need not speak to communicate certain feelings or emotions.

I guess they know. I can tell them later what I've done. I'll suggest to Suzie she does similar with Timothy's listings on her cell phone…

All of us glance up and stare at the lift when it announces Suzie's arrival. She walks towards us holding a can of cola and looks surprised when she sees a coffee table decked out with various food and drink.

"We brought plenty of food if you're also hungry," Jake explains, nodding towards the table.

Suzie grins, quickly dives around the table and sits down next to me. She beams at me, then flashes me a wink - our agreed signal that the 'deed' is done. Neither of the others sitting there would be told what it was we'd done, as agreed, but I'm certain they can guess well enough…

Especially now the loser boyfriends have upped and stomped off, I think.

Jake's cell phone rings, and he answers it. After a minute he hangs up, "Unless they've teamed up for some childish hide n seek they're nowhere in the theatre," he grunts. "I guess we can go after they have done the judging…"

Suzie and I glance at one another. Not from surprise that the loser boyfriends are gone, but to find out the judging of the audition will happen soon… or so it seems. We glance back at each of our respective notebook like we're two school kids caught out exchanging answers in an exam.

The silence in the office is deafening, then we both jerk when Jake rises from his chair walks from the room.

I guess he's off to use the restroom. I watch him walk to the lift.

Once Jake is gone, it's more obvious why he left. Liz decides it's time for girlie talk.

+++

Liz gets up, and she walks to her desk and retrieves a bag from it.

She moves some packaging out of the way, then empties the bag's content. A pile of several dozen magazines spill out in a disorderly heap. Suzie and I glance at each other than both of us dive for different magazines.

"I think you've done enough song writing for today. I think you need some relaxation now," Liz says warmly, almost motherly. "There's a reason for this. I want you to keep hold of a pen and circle clothing, furniture, adverts, anything that appeals to you. It will be a way for me to assess your likes quickly and for us to figure out things you'd wear when you join me at my concert. That will happen regardless of whether the results later are in your favour or otherwise…"

"What if we have different tastes?" Suzie asks.

"Styles and tastes can be adapted easily," Liz answers. "For example, you might think I always wear such boring trouser suits such this…"

Suzie and I both nod at the same time.

"In fact, when I'm at home my style is more hippy," Liz continues. "When I'm on tour, I wear long flowing dresses…"

"I've only ever heard you on the radio," I say. "I never even thought of going to one of your concerts… Sorry…"

"Perfectly fine," Liz says. "People are often surprised by the different personalities Liz James brings along with her based on what I'm doing. For this audition they wanted judges, who are well versed in the industry, but that those auditioning might never have heard of."

"Hence why you didn't want me to reveal your identity earlier…" I say.

"Precisely that," Liz says. "There are a lot of other reasons too, some to do with keeping me safe from fans who might be like that one of years ago."

"Where is he now?" Suzie asks. "If I'm allowed to ask."

"They convicted him of stalking and sent to jail for six years," Liz says flatly. "I heard he took his own life a year into his internment. Jake is… somewhat protective me despite that happening. That's why he left. He's doing the rounds despite the theatre being all locked up now. I guess he's rattled about how Mick had shouted at me after you'd left…"

"I don't think he will bother Tash any more," Suzie says. "I sorted that out for sure…"

I glance at Suzie, frowning for a moment. She hadn't told me any details yet about what happened between them, but then I realise I hadn't done it either. I guess the silence from Liz is because she notices tension between us.

"I've called around and made some arrangements for both of you over the next few months," Liz continues using a sharper tone than before to pull my attention back to herself. "I presume that you'll make living arrangements if you find this friend of yours. And then there's the matter of study. I want you both to become as knowledgeable of the industry as I am. See it as a scholarship."

Suzie and I gape at one another. I doubt either of us had arrived here a few weeks earlier with the idea that we might end up with all the things that Liz was now throwing at us. It proves to us she's a generous person, and that she knew it when she saw real talent. She'd obviously decided that both of were equally talented. It's also clear this decision wasn't conditioned on us getting through the final part of the auditions.

"For us both?" I ask sheepishly.
"If your plan definitely is for you to work together, and I've seen enough to know you're well suited together in personality and in how your work ethics seem to match so well," Liz answers. "Then also use this time to learn about one another more. The more you know each other, the higher your chances at success will be."
We nod to show we agree. We glance at each other's choice of magazine. It's as telling as how we present ourselves. When we'd met, I'd been wearing my hat all the time with my unruly long curly hair tumbling loose; Suzie's hair was tightly fastened in a bun and she'd been wearing her make-up meticulously…

As I stare at Suzie, I notice she's changed. The make-up has gone and just a small streak of eye-liner is present. Rather than having her hair in a bun, her hair is now in a short ponytail.

Suzie grins at me because it shows how much I'd occupied myself with my work, then she reaches out and grabs my hat and places it on her own head. "Suits you..." I quip at her, grinning.

"I might buy me one," Suzie says.

"It's easier to pull off the look with loose hair..." I say, then I grin broadly as Suzie pulls her hair from the ponytail and replaces the hat. Her hair isn't as long as mine, but once it's loose, she appears younger.

"I'm guessing you two are settling on the cowgirl look," Liz guesses.

We nod then grin at one another and then beam a grin at Liz. For the moment we have nothing to worry about or to annoy us, and this conversation with Liz distracts us also from having to talk about what was really on our mind - what we'd done earlier with Timothy and Mick...

We both seem to fumble with the magazines and seem to feel shy for several minutes. Suzie takes off my hat and gives it back to me. Rather than replacing it on my head, I place it on the sofa beside me. I too can do things differently in terms of appearance. Glancing towards Suzie I notice that now her hair isn't tightly combed back it wants to fall around her face in curls...

I feel Liz's eyes probing me for answers she's won't get from us. She'd said that as much earlier. I pretend to be reading the magazine I've opened on a random page. The face of a bearded old man stares back at me, sporting an enigmatic smile, reminding me somewhat of my late grandfather before he'd died. I look at the title of the article and discover I've opened the magazine to an article about some businessman who'd started his business late in life.

Smart thing for him to do. It's never too late to do something new...

I circle the face of the man with my pen, and a quick glance sidelong tells me that Suzie is curious about what I might be reading. Her eyebrow raising for a moment tells me she's now curious why I'd circle some old dude in the magazine.

"Reminds me of my grandpa," I write beside the face in case she's still looking. The note will also help Liz later on to get a better idea of what sort of things I valued from family life. After reading through the article twice, and it giving me some ideas how to finish one of my songs, I turn the page and I'm staring at a fashion shoot at a catwalk show.

I study every person carefully, circling those who wear clothes I'd definitely would be wearing. I circle a tiny circle on one woman, draw an arrow and write, "Just the necklace on this one."

Yeah, if Liz wants us doing this I will do it seriously and make sure she learns as much as she can about me...

I glance sideways and see that Suzie is as busy with her magazine. The occasional snort explains to me what she's likely reading right now.

I glance at the table and determine there are likely over a hundred magazines there, and a few newspapers too that I think that were bought for Jake to read, and I'm getting an idea in my mind how life is for someone like Liz James with a successful career, recording business, a record label that she can offer to artists such as Suzie and myself, and probably thousands of different endorsements and sources of income. I resist the temptation to grab my cell phone to check whether Liz has written any books, and my mind already decides that I'd write a book about her if she had no biography yet. The more I think about what Liz has told us about herself, about the amazing and occasionally terrifying life she's led, the more I'm convinced I want the SAME...

I turn another page. It shows the advert for my favourite perfume. I hesitate a moment, then I circle the entire page and write, "Plenty please," on the corner of the page. I draw a smile beside it before glancing up at Liz. I notice now she's also reading a magazine. It's a magazine about country music. I decide that I have to look for another such magazine in the mountain of magazines in front of me. Country music is my father's favourite music and one reason I enjoy wearing the cowboy hat that's lying on the sofa beside me.

For a moment I glance around feeling aware of Jake missing from the room and guess that he's checking that all the doors are securely shut together with 'Collin' and whoever else was around of the staff still. Security staff are still here to keep the building safe whenever it's not in use…

I turn my attention back to the magazine and have to keep myself from grinning or giggling when I realise it's an article about Liz I'm now reading. Now the tables are turned. Now I can learn more about her. I take her words to be literal and pretend I'm doing some assignment for uni and start underlining the sentences of her answers I like. The more I read the article, the more my respect for the woman opposite of me grows, and the more I like her as a friend…

Chapter Twenty-One

Once Jake is back, I think that Liz and he want some private time for themselves as they silently get up, throw away their empty bags and containers and walk to the furthest corner of the office; it's a part of the office I hadn't even been aware of up to now because it had been bathed in darkness. A light flicks on for a moment, Jake busies himself with laying out some pillows on two of the sofas there and drapes a blanket on each. I guess they often use the office to sleep. There's no point to leave the theatre until we were planning to go home… wherever home was for the other individuals around me. For me, home was a dingy motel room six blocks from here.

Unless I find Tommy. Unless I go home with Tommy…

Suzie nudges me after we're alone. I glance at her.

"Did you have fun with him?" she asks.

It surprises me she'd even ask me the question, and after a minute and few more nudges I nod my head. I sincerely dread the next question would be about what I did to *or* with Timothy, but I stare incredulously because of what Suzie says next about my ex-boyfriend. Something that shocks me more than I let her know.

"We just sat there and talked," she says. "He admitted something to me…"

"Oh, what?" I ask hesitantly.

"Did you know he's bisexual," Suzie says.

"Bi… errr… no," I say. "He has never told me ever…"

"Apparently, he had a crush on the drummer who *slept* with you at the last gig in a pub," Suzie continues. "He said the last time you were a back-up singer was two years ago... He said that if I even talked about it with you you'd know which one I meant if I said to you it's where he argued with the drummer and then gave him a black eye..."

"Errr... that's right," I say glumly.

"Apparently, he'd been going to the gig for over three weeks before you arrived and tried - and failed - to chat up the guy... I think he said the guy's name is Nicolas," Suzie says. "He claimed to me he was doing all the sex with you to cure himself from his... errr... bi-ness... as he'd stated to me. There's more if you're up to hearing it..."

"Go ahead," I whisper.

"He... he said he wanted to play you for a fool, and somehow dump you if you didn't get in," Suzie says. "He wanted to make life hell for you and take every cent you make for himself..."

I grunt audibly from the seething anger I now feel towards Mick. I'd been guessing for months about why he'd been standoffish towards me and then would manipulate me with sex or his kinks at the worst moments.

"I don't think he realised that your songs belong legally to you," Suzie continues. "I didn't tell him about it."

"His behaviour explains why he disappeared for a few days at a time from time to time," I grunt.

"I claimed that if things didn't work out, he could find someone else," Suzie says. "Then he tried to make a move on me but by the time he finished talking I felt uncomfortable around him..."

Suzie runs her hand over her loose hair and continues, "The reason I wore it loose is based on what he'd said about me. He claimed that I looked *too* much like a boy with my hair tied flat against my head. And said that I looked like a mannequin with my makeup. I was washing it off when you texted me..."

"He's a bully about people's appearances to be honest," I say. "I guess now you understand what I said about me not wearing any..."

"I guess so..." Suzie admits. "I never realised how terrible of a person he really was. I'm so sorry. Had I known better, I wouldn't have suggested the *plan*. But what about Timothy...?"

She had uttered the dreaded question.

"After what you just told me I'm not sure if I can tell you what happened with me," I whisper, feeling upset now.

"Actually, I don't want to know… never tell me," Suzie blurts out. "I agree with Liz now that it's best that certain things aren't known. But I think you needed to be told to make you see that being with Tommy is the best option for you…"

"Yes, that's also something my father told me whenever I had a bad day at school," I whisper. "He says the truth can hurt but that it can also make it easier afterwards to make the correct decisions. If I hadn't met you in the restroom that day I wouldn't be sitting here dreaming of a better, an easier future with someone who now regard as my best friend. And I've not had that many friends in my life as I've always been on the move…"

"So it means that if the news from Liz is that we've won the audition and if the news from my friend is that she's found Tommy that's the icing on the cake," Suzie whispers. "A massive chocolate cake with a lot of After Eight mints decking it for my sweet tooth…"

Suzie shows me the open page of the latest magazine she's paging through. It's an advertisement for the chocolate. My mouth waters…

"I like them too," I admit.

"Then we'll demand we have two crates full of them for us at every concert we perform in," Suzie says resolutely, which causes me to laugh loudly and which breaks the gloomy atmosphere that had settled between us.

After a few minutes, Suzie seems determined to change the topic, "What do you think our chances are?"

"I hope we get in, but you heard Liz. She'll accept us at her record label even if they say no," I answer, grinning again, and then I hold up the magazine I had placed next to me. "See if there's a second one of this magazine on the table. It has an article about Liz in it. If you find it, read it, underline things you find interesting and when we're alone, later we'll compare notes…"

Suzie divides for the pile of magazines like they're Christmas gifts.

"Found it," she shrieks. "Oh my god, she looks so young in these photos…"

"Read it," I say. "I think it meant us to find Liz. Her story mostly is so similar to what we've been through. I admire her so much now. She's like the mother who wasn't ever there for me in my mind. She's like someone who cares about what I want to achieve in life. I told you before that my mother isn't much involved in my life. She was the reason for the argument between Brianna and myself and we both blame for causing it. Read it, please... You might understand me more too because of it... And who knows, maybe I can convince Brianna to write a book called Pretty In Blue all about our journey to success..."

"I'd like that..."

+++

After two hours, Suzie and I are startled by the appearance of Liz, who sits down on the edge of the coffee table beside us. She leans closer and whispers - obviously so not to wake up Jake who we can hear snoring from across the room.

"I have to go now because we will do the judging," Liz whispers. "I'll be back in about three hours if you're not successful. If you are successful, there will be a phone call. It will be someone else who calls you. Whatever they say in the call is something you should listen to closely."

We nod.

Liz gets up, glances at each of us for a whole minute, then she nods, turns around and walks to the lift. After another two minutes Suzie and I are alone with a sleeping Jake in the furthest corner.

We glance at each other than at the window frame we'd used earlier to sit and talk, and work on the music. Now we sit there to make certain we aren't disturbing Jake.

At the same time we lean over and glance at the sleeping man and Suzie goes, "Ahh..." like she's looking at a baby in its cot. We chuckle softly, get up and are sitting opposite of each other with a few cushions behind each of our backs. Once I've made myself comfortable, I glance again across the square and study the building

I'd deemed ugly a few hours earlier.

But now, with the lights decorating the outside turned on, it takes on a rustic beauty. I stare specifically at a window on the second floor for an odd reason, like I can will its occupant to reveal themselves to me.

"Why do you keep looking at the building?" Suzie asks.

"I don't know," I answer. "Something draws me to it. I feel like I should want to be there for an odd reason."

I shrug my shoulders and turn my attention forcefully to my notebook. To the four words written there...

"Love lost, love gained..."

I'd written the words just before I'd turned away from the window, looking out at the square. I glance at Suzie from the corner of my eye, and I see her peering aimlessly from the window, deep in thought. I think it had disturbed her that she had to tell me about Mick. I glance down at the paper once again, grab hold of my pen and move it several times over the first two words.

"Suzie," I whisper, looking up at her once more.

She turns her head after a minute and I can see it glazes her eyes in the dim light of the late afternoon.

"Yes," she says plainly.

I hold up my notebook towards her with my writing and say, "Let's concentrate on that part and forget about them, okay?"

Suzie seems to contemplate my words for the longest time, then she nods.

"Brianna might be my sister by birth but I regard you almost like a sister too," I continue.

A wistful smile appears on Suzie's face. As an only child, the concept of having sisters is new to her. To have an adopted sister who'd encourage her creative endeavours would do her good.

"One other thing," I say next. "Once we've found Tommy, don't put yourself off true love. YOU are the reason I even find him again. Who knows... there might be a right guy for you out there too and you don't even know it yet..."

"I'll remember that," Suzie says, now smiling happier, but still showing the glaze of tears in her eyes; hopefully any tears that would come would be happy tears for a newly found family, a positive future for us as musicians, and maybe also because she tried to help someone find her true love…

"We won't see them again," Suzie continues. "I know I said I want to be single. Maybe for a while I'll do that, but then—"

My cell phone going off loudly startles both Suzie and myself so much that we jump up from the window frame we're using as seating.

I stare at the phone that vibrates loudly because of where it had been placed. The usual jingle used to alert me of phone calls sounds unworldly and odd to my ears. The sound produced can easily belong in the soundtrack of some horror B-Movie. I cock my head and listen to it for a moment. The other part of my mind that comes up with musical scores for my songs suddenly realises that this odd-sounding tune will be perfect for one of my weirder songs…

A nudge in my ribs distracts me. I glance sidelong at Suzie with an annoyed frown on my face, "Pick it up, you stupid idiot of a bint." The words make me more annoyed but Suzie grins at me and makes it clear she's just teasing me, "If you don't I will, and I'll pretend to be you…"

"NO!" I almost shout the word and I dive for my phone.

"McKinsey—yes, hello…" I blurt out with an undertone of laughter in my voice.

Part of me wants to be polite, the other part wants to be informal. I listen to a voice explaining certain pieces of information that I probably would have to have repeated to me later on. As I listen to the voice on the other end of the phone call, I realise something extraordinary has just happened to my life…

+++

"WHO was that?" Suzie asks abruptly as I place my phone back into my bag. I stare at her wide-eyed, and I'm unable to speak for several minutes. My heart pounds as hard as it did just before the audition. I'm in shock and I can't believe I was just told. Never in all my life have I had news such as this that will forever alter my life.

"It was…" I say but my mouth goes dry and the next few words don't want to come out.

"WHO was it?" Suzie says with more force and it snaps me from my daze.

"I'm in… errr… we're in… errr… we've got it… errr… Rose Petals," I stammer before I giggle and I jump around before I land myself in the nearest chair feeling so overjoyed that I cannot say anything other repeat four words over and over.

For the moment all the gloomy nature of our conversation about Mick and Timothy is all but forgotten…

Chapter Twenty-Two

After all the hassles and all the mayhem of the last ten days I know now that the next phone call to my sister Brianna will be a happy one. I can tell her I'm going to BE a real artist like Liz James. I doubt she'll believe me right now if I tell her I'm signed up with her label. Well, almost - as I still have a pesky contract to fix that, according to both Liz and Suzie, needs fixing in a serious way. I'd done a good enough job fumbling through the legal knowledge learned from my father to make it not as disastrous as it could have been had it been the way that Mick wanted it…

I check my phone for the time and consider for a moment whether to call my father, but then I'd be on the phone for many hours having to explain why I hadn't been in touch for so long. It would raise awkward questions too, as he'd known about Tommy - or more precisely, Thomas.

He probably thinks we're married, has a bunch of grandkids running around who don't know him and who wants to see urgently…

I grab the contract from the table on the terrace where I'd ended up after Suzie said she had a few things to do. She took her phone so I'm guessing she was in the middle of orchestrating some surprise for me. She said I deserved a surprise…

+++

I'm believing more and more that today has been a weird day if I think it over. Now that I look back, I think this has been the weirdest two weeks of my entire life. Endless hours waiting in the queue for the auditions to open, staring at the array of different artists and talent that had stood there too. Then for them to select me from among with a thousand others...

What the fuck... was it a thousand people that they had to listen to. Pour Liz, no wonder she's exhausted. How could she cope with all that...?

I pack my notebooks and folder containing the music contract into my bag. I run my hand over the light leather. It had been a gift - well, the only one in the last decade - from my mother. Despite the not-so-mutual feelings between us, I still valued a gift like this from her. I still love her, despite the way she had caused problems between Brianna and me.

I lean forward and look over the large square to check if I can see Suzie anywhere. I wave when from the left she's walking towards me fast, and she's on the phone like she'd been a lot in the last two hours, even getting a momentary annoyed stare from Liz when she and Jake left to go home and had tried to say goodbye to Suzie.

I grab the handful of music sheets I'd purchased in a nearby shop a few days ago and read through the notes as memories come flooding back of me doing the same with my grandmother who'd noticed my talent for singing and music before anyone else. She had taught me this skill. After five minutes, I place them back in my bag when I see Suzie walking towards me finally... and she puts her cell phone in her bag.

I grunt about her not being on her phone of all the times she could have done this...

"How's things going with you?" Suzie asks, smiling teasingly at me.

I grunt again—loudly! And I hear a snort as a response to it, meaning that Suzie knows I'm getting increasingly more annoyed with her.

So damned annoying she is right now…

+++

My unexpected journey from an unknown, semi-homeless girl travelling from gig to gig trying to escape a past, had ended up with everything that had happened today and that I had done - which, like the last few days, had started so simple, and maybe with me being *too* gullible for my good., and with me STILL believing *too* much that Mick would help me gain the career I wanted, and then having to dismiss the idea as I walked to the audition on my own.

I'd arrived at this theatre with Mick in tow with the goal of taking part in the auditions and looking back the last few days it had turned all out differently than I had expected. The odd choice of entrusting two other women with the knowledge of my life situation had unexpected side effects or results.

However, if I look at it closer, it was these two individuals who'd helped shape my life to begin a new phase, for my life to go differently.

From what I note based on the vague comments that come from Suzie beside me - the few done purposely in English - towards her Polish friend whose voice I recognise now, I'm realising that it is *three* women altering my destiny and my love life for good. I think something is definitely happening, and that's why Suzie is so mysterious suddenly…

Gleefully I think actually I need to update my assessment of what's going on with my life when I add another person to the list, *Four women if I were to count in Brianna in this oddball list and she gets the credit being the person who'd got me to become a singer. If it had never been for the argument.*

I frown when my demented brain adds another person… my grandmother.

Well, maybe she's responsible for the genes…

Then I grunt when I realise my sister I would never have argued if my mother wasn't part of this stupid puzzle I'm creating...

"Everything okay?" Suzie asks.

Suzie seems so distracted now by the phone call she accepts a grunt as an answer...

+++

Thirty minutes later it seems all of Suzie's desire to use her cell phone has evaporated and she and I watch the sky with our heads leaning back, like we're two tourists enjoying the last remnants of a warm day. After the busy day, being so relaxed and mellowed out is almost like a luxury.

"Isn't this heaven?" Suzie whispers.

I grunt again, now more to be teasing Suzie for a change. She seems to ignore it so I answer, "Yeah, it is. Just wondering what I will do with the rest of the day..."

I glance sidelong for a response that never comes.

I bet she's messing with my mind after all the stuff I said about Timothy. I guess I deserved her ignoring me this somewhat...

But I know it's all a tease, anyway. From the fact that she'd spoken several times now in what I understand to be Polish - and I'd checked it on Google to mean 'hello' and my only knowledge so far of the convoluted language I'm realising that this it!

She's likely talking to her friend who will soon tell her she's been unsuccessful and then break the sad new to me a moment later...

Yeah, my brain can be rather sarcastic with me in moments such as this. I'm already being fatalistic about the success because, as usual, having one bit of good luck land in one's lap is one thing but to have TWO good things happen is another...

Or three, if you count Liz. Or four, if you also include the spectacular boyfriend DUMP. A perfectly executed DUMP, really. And a lot of fun, too…

I smirk with obvious delight at the last part. I'd suspected for months that something was up with Mick, but I never guess it would be because he's bisexual. Not that I got anything against anyone who is because I got several friends whose sofas I had crashed on over the years who are gay. My smirk becomes bigger when I realise I'd send a super-funny mixed message to Mick because of it.

I guess he had so many reasons to want to get back at me, yet I did to him first because of Suzie…

"What's so funny?" Suzie asks.

"Mick is…" I answer, giggling loudly.

"Huh what? Is the idiot back or something?" Suzie asks, looking around the square, panicked.

"Naah, he's long gone," I reply. "I just realised I had fooled him so much over the years and never realised how much fun I could have had if I had realised about him being bisexual sooner…"

"Oh right," Suzie says, closing her eyes once more. And briefly smirking.

"How is the phone calling going?" I purr at Suzie, knowing I won't get a straight answer out of her about it anyway, but because suddenly my mood has improved a thousandfold, I'm not fazed about her not telling me about their purpose.

After another twenty minutes have passed, I've all but given up about getting an answer out of Suzie, and I shut my eyes and pretend to sleep. Even when she calls out my name repeatedly to determine if I'm asleep or pretending to be asleep.

I go with the latter option until she goes quiet…

Suzie's phone loudly ringing interrupts the silence and our occasional distorted conversation. It's obvious that we're both equally startled by the sound of it ringing loudly.

Suzie dives for the phone and after listening to her friend—who has to speak to Suzie in Polish now of all times when she could speak English instead. I notice Suzie glancing at me a few times as she listens intently, then she announces in English teasingly, "It's my friend. She has some news for us... Well, actually for YOU, sweetie..."

Suzie grabs my arm as she listens on her cell phone, nodding profusely. She holds me rather forcefully as far away from her phone as she can with me becoming impatient really quickly.

She smiles a few times at me but every time that I try to ask Suzie something the phone call she purposefully pushes me from her, steps back a few feet, and shuts me up by holding me in an iron grip once again...

+++

Once Suzie hangs up the phone and I can speak with her about whatever it had been about, I feel like a kid waiting to open her Christmas presents, and I feel just as excited and energetic as I might have felt back then...

She stares intently at me for several minutes, studying me for my reactions to the phone call, and also teasing me. She's not in any hurry to put me out of my misery...

"AND...?" I ask, almost shouting my question at her. "AND?" I repeat a few seconds later, much louder.

"Hush it... Okay, I'll tell you what's going on. SHE has found him..." Suzie says plainly. "And it will be easy enough for YOU to go meet him in person and be with him to sort things out between the two of you..."

"How come?" I ask sheepishly.

"Because he lives, and he works in THIS very city, you silly bint," Suzie answers. "In fact, we're located right opposite of his workplace," Suzie points across the square at a familiarly looking building that's now half-bathed in the beginnings of dusk. "He's over there so get your old boyfriend back, you bint, and the lady that I just spoke to says she's expecting you…"

+++

Suzie points at a specific building across the square from the theatre. It's the same building that, when I arrived here, I'd thought of as ugly when I'd stared at for several minutes after watching Timothy walking away. I grin for a moment that it's ironic for me to end up doing an audition so close where Tommy could be found. Suddenly, I feel the need to believe that some people are just meant to be together.

Yeah, maybe the irony won't be lost when I tell about to Brianna and she'll write her next book about chance visit where two people who'd been in love and who find each other again…

Chapter Twenty-Three

Now, suddenly, the ugliest building of the city is in my mind one of the best-looking building in the whole city or even the whole world. It's where Tommy is according to Suzie's explanation that seemed to come from far away…

"Do you mind if I go there to see if he's really there, and if he remembers me. Can you keep hold of my bag so I can get there quicker," I ask. "If all fails I can claim I'm looking for somewhere to have a meal…"

"Go for it," Suzie says, smiling. "If all fails I'll be waiting here for you…"

I smile once at Suzie, then sprint to the other side of the square while behind me Suzie is cheering me on like I'm running the marathon right now. I ignore the fact that a moment later TWO voices are doing this to me…

+++

I stop abruptly a few minutes later and I stare up at the signage on the building and my grin broadens even more. To discover Tommy has some sort of job in a law firm that deals with the entertainment industry - *my* line of work now I got accepted for the casting cal, the next part of the audition process, I'd hoped to secure - for *us* in fact as Rose Petals, it's time for me to dump the useless lawyer that Mick had chosen…

"In with the new, out with the old…" I mumble.

I hope the words are true. Even if the words only applied to dumping Mick as a boyfriend a few hours ago. Now I hope the same to be true in terms of a boyfriend and a new lawyer. Suzie's friend said Tommy is single…

I open the door and walk inside. A woman in her mid-forties looks up from the reception desk on the left.

"I'm here to speak with Tommy Charlton," I hiss. "I'm an old friend of his…"

"Tommy—" she echoes the name like she's not familiar with it. For a few moments I wonder if Suzie's friend got the wrong person. Then my heart beats faster, "Mr Charlton is out for lunch but he's due back, well, he's supposed to be back already. Let me call up and see if he's in his office. Who can I say is asking for him?"

"Tell him it's Tash McKinsey… or if he doesn't remember me, tell him it's the girl who walked off and never came back…"

I listen hard for his voice as the receptionist relays my message. She hangs up the phone, then points towards the chairs to her right, "You can wait there. He's on his way down…"

As I wait, my mind races over all the things I want to say to him. I don't get a long time for it when a familiar voice rings out, "Tash…"

I look up and stare at Tommy. He has changed little since the last time we'd been in the same room. I get up and I'm about to say any of the million things I want to tell him, but before I get a chance for questions, explanations or whatever else I want to say, I have his lips over mine. He kisses me passionately like there had been no passage of time between the last time we were this close and right now.

After a few minutes Tommy abruptly pulls himself away from me, and he looks me over. He looks as emotional as I'm feeling right now…

"I'm sorry…" I stammer.

"For what?" Tommy asks.

"For walking off like I did…" I reply.

"I guess we can make up for lost time now you're back…" he says.

"You're not angry…" I say glumly.

"Why would I be? I knew you had dreams you wanted to pursue. I would have impeded them," Tommy breathes. "Did you fulfil those dreams…?"

"Almost… errr—" I say, and glance sidelong towards the receptionist who seems to want to pretend to be working, but her body language shows she's actually aware of what's going on between Tommy and I.

"In case you wonder who this is…" Tommy says. His voice makes both the receptionist and I jump up with surprise. "Do you remember Aunt Maggie…? You've never met her, right? Now you have…"

"Do you mean to say that this is the girl you've been pining for… for all this time…" Maggie grunts. Now she's been outed as someone who knows Tommy even better than she'd made out. "He talks all the time about going to find you, and then you find him first. How did you know he's here?"

"Actually, it's a friend and my new band member who's responsible for it," I answer before Tommy can say anything. "She's apparently a private investigator of some sort…"

"I guess that explains the phone call three days ago…" Maggie grunts. "Must have been that private investigator…"

"I didn't know she'd be this fast in tracking you down," I say. "But am I right in thinking you work here in this law firm… errr…"

Suddenly, I feel shy as I look from person to person, hoping they'll guess what I want from Tommy besides a rekindled friendship or, if possible, the original love we felt before.

Tommy takes hold of me firmly and looks me over once more, then he asks, "Is something going on that I should know about?"

"Well, it's the fact that in a single day I get the music career I want, the contract for a record with a new friend, find you, discover that my old contract for my band name is shitty as hell, broke up with an as shitty boyfriend, discover I love you still..."

I stop speaking abruptly when I realise what I just said.

"I may help with the contract..." Tommy says reassuringly. He seems to ignore the rest of what I said apart from the part about the record deal. "I presume you have a legal agreement of some sort between the two of you about the band...?"

"The lawyer representing the theatre helped with that..." I answer. "But he said we got to do something about the old contract. It has—it has the signature of my old boyfriend on it and I don't want him involved with my career in any way..."

"You HELP them, Tommy..." Maggie interjects forcefully. "She seems nice enough and any 'ex' would only impede the two of you down the road... Especially, if you will still do what you told me you'd do whenever you'd found her. Well, you've found her. For once listen to your Aunt Maggie when she tells you something..."

I stare from Maggie to Tommy and back to Maggie. His mannerisms are so similar to those I remember to be Tommy's mannerisms...

"I guess Aunt Maggie has revealed I'm a lawyer, and in case you didn't guess it yet I also work in the entertainment industry. In fact, I represent artists and musicians," Tommy explains. "Your desire to work in this industry also was a catalyst for my choice of career... well, at least it became that choice after a good talking down from Aunt Maggie..."

Maggie laughs loudly at the accusation, "Well, are you going to make sure it reassures her, or just stand there with her?"

"Yes, yes, you're right," Tommy says. "Please come with me, Tash. My office is on the first floor. Do you have anyone waiting for you?"

"My band mate Suzie is waiting for me, but she said that if I was successful here, she wouldn't mind waiting for me..." I say.

"Where is she waiting?" Tommy asks.

"At the cafeteria next to the theatre..." I answer.

"I can get my paperwork and then we meet up with her as she'd need to sign things too," Tommy says then he runs up the stairs as fast as he might have done years earlier.

+++

Maggie glances from person to person for a moment before she speaks, "Some things don't change," and Maggie glances after Tommy as he walks off quickly. "He was always a good athlete, but music is his passion because of his deep feelings for *you*, Tash..."

I nod in agreement, then smile at Maggie. If there was one person here who might be responsible for the good chance of Tommy and I getting back together, it would be Maggie. She'd encouraged his pursuit of finding me.

"I think I realised I love him after talking with Suzie yesterday..." I say firmly. "I wanted to find him because of it..."

"Are you here to stay?" Maggie asks.

"Yes, I am..." I answer. "I realised I made an error in judgement when I left him before... As I walked here I realised I missed him a lot..."

"He missed you..." Maggie continues. "It bemused me when he chose this city as the choice for these offices. It means a thirty-minute commute for me, but now I think it's worth it all..."

I smile when I hear speedy footsteps rushing down the stairs. Only a moment later and he's standing in front of me, panting loudly, clutching a thick bundle of paperwork with his left arm and holding a briefcase in his right hand.

"Are you ready?" Tommy asks, sounding bemused and curious at the same time.

I nod.

"Okay, let's meet up with your friend..." Tommy says. "I have paperwork for both of you to sign that would make me your legal counsel in relation to your careers..."

I nod once more.

Maggie waves goodbye as we walk from the office building. As we walk across the square Tommy leans sideways and kisses my forehead, then says the words I've been longing to hear for the past five days ever since Suzie's friend had started her work to find him...

"I love you, Tash McKinsey..."

"I love you too, Tommy Charlton…"

"I guess as I already proposed before that I can suggest to you we could get married this coming summer if you're okay with it," Tommy continues. "If you want to…"

"Yes, that would be nice…" I breathe. "I would want that very much…"

I feel my steps become lighter, my heart beat faster, and a smile forming on my face. As we get closer to the cafeteria, I see Suzie sitting there with a woman opposite of her. We walk inside, and finally I meet the person who has helped to give me back my true love…

I wave at Suzie and I beam at her, "… So, this is Tommy I presume…" Suzie says warmly, eyeing Tommy for several minutes. "You have a good catch there, Tash. Don't let the catch go again like you did before. In case you wonder, this is Angela Jameson and she's who found the love of your life for you…"

I shake Angela's hand. She shakes Tommy's hand too.

"I'm guessing your aunt gave you a shock of your life…" Angela says, smiling teasingly at Tommy. I look up at Tommy. He blushes, then he smiles at me. I smile back at him. He swallows hard, then he explains why he's here with me.

"Tash said there was a contract I needed to check over and fix…"

"Yes, apparently both her former manager and my former manager seem to think they can control our career," Suzie says coldly. "I called Angela when they came here and annoyed me…"

"He's here now," I say. "We'll be okay now…"

I take Tommy's hand and stare at the pile of paperwork he holds against his chest.

"Yes, right," Tommy comments. "Let's sit down and go over the paperwork and also show me the contract I need to serve the court next week. So I can make sure the two gentlemen can never interfere with your careers and private lives…"

"I might help with gathering evidence," Angela interjects.

"Tash told me about you," Tommy says, nodding affirmatively. "If you visit my office next Monday, you can speak with Maggie and work with her on fact finding…"

"Let's order drinks to celebrate everything we achieved today," Suzie suggests. "What do you all want to drink…?"

"Cola…"

Tommy and I glance at one another as we'd said the word at the same time; we both grin at the fact that in reality we're still so similar in our tastes.

"Yes, I think I will be okay now…" I whisper. "And now I think about everything that's happened to us, it just feels like we're all caught up in some big cliche…"

"You mean also a stupid cliche about two women breaking into the entertainment industry?" Suzie asks. "It almost seems too good to be true…"

I nod then I gesture towards Tommy, "And the obvious cliche of the handsome guy saving them…"

The End